To read more stories by Dakota Caldwell
please visit
www.leadpyramidpublishing.com

Apocolyps Squad

Squad

Dakota Caldwell

Dakota Caldwell
8152 Marty St.
Overland Park, KS 66204
www.leadpyramidpublishing.com

cover design copyright © 2019: Alexiss Eastman-Edmonds

Printed in the United States of America

ISBN: 978-1-947155-08-4

First printing, 2019

Acknowledgements

To my wife, Jordan, who for reasons unknown to myself still reads everything I write. To my incredible daughter, Willow, who brings more joy to my life than a five-star review.

An enormous thanks to Alexiss Eastman-Edmonds for putting together the fantastic cover, and helping me figure out what my characters looked like!

And, as always, to my Lord and Savior Jesus Christ. May his light always stand against the monsters in our own lives.

CHAPTER 0

"Sir!" A young private leapt out of the rescue helicopter and tore across the sandy soil of the Nevada desert. "We need to get out of here!"

General Herford took a deep breath and slowly turned away from the mouth of the cave entrance. "If we aren't dead yet, we aren't going to die. No need for running."

"Sir?" The private drew up short as he reached the entrance of the cave. The General could only imagine the shock at unexpectedly seeing hundreds of dead bodies littering the ground. "Oh-"

"Turns out that this little insurgency was a bit larger than we thought." General Herford chose his words carefully. There was no way that anyone could know what had actually transpired on the mountain, not if the country was going to remain stable. "A lot of good men died today."

"What…" The private choked for a moment. "What happened? We knew there was a rebel group here, but I thought you were going to be able to take them easily enough."

"What's your name, private?"

The soldier snapped to attention immediately. "Private Jefferson, sir."

"I assume that you're new."

"Yes, sir."

"Then there's something that you should know." General Herford sighed and stroked his beard. "Never ask a commanding officer what happened after a battle. You may not want to know that answer."

"Yes, sir."

General Herford waited a moment longer before nodding. "Alright. We can go now."

As he climbed into the helicopter, he took one last glance at the forbidden mountain. They had gone in knowing that a simple group of discontented citizens had gotten their hands on military-grade equipment and challenged the government. What they had found… Herford was privately glad that no one else had survived the onslaught. Fewer mouths to keep shut.

Well, *almost* no one else had survived. Though he couldn't see it, Herford knew that one other helicopter was flying away from the battle. If any of his superiors, or even his inferiors, knew who that survivor was, he would be court-marshaled in an instant.

He only hoped that he hadn't made a mistake trusting the man. Only time would tell, he supposed. His only hope was to hold up his end of the bargain and hope beyond hope that his newfound partner came through.

If either of them failed… Well, neither of them would live long enough to regret it.

CHAPTER 1

FIVE YEARS LATER...

"As you can see, we run a tight ship around here." Aaron bowed low before the inspector. "Not a thing out of order."

"Well, so far, I'm inclined to agree with that assessment." The inspector breezed past the hapless bureaucrat. "That said, we've only just finished looking over the waiting room. If you don't mind, I'd like to take a look at your secretary's office."

Aaron paused. "Sir, I'm really not sure that-"

"Are you trying to hide something?" The inspector slid his glasses down his nose, freezing Aaron in his tracks.

Aaron did his best to look innocent, shook his head, and waved at a door that led out of the waiting room. As he opened the door, he took a deep breath.

It wasn't that he wasn't ready for an inspector. In fact, he and his team had a number of incredibly detailed procedures regarding the presence of a government inspection. The only problem was that the Monarchs game was on, and their security guard was in the break room with the rest of the faculty. The only reason Aaron had managed to meet the inspector was due to an incredibly well-timed restroom break.

"As I'm sure you know, the results of this inspection will determine how much funding you receive during the next four quarters." The inspector droned on in a monotone voice, and Aaron stroked his beard. "Do you mind stating for the record just what it is you do here?"

"I thought you already had that information." Aaron swallowed. "Besides, I thought we were looking at the secretary's office."

By now, they had reached the end of the small hallway that Aaron had led them down. The inspector glanced at the door, which was just as dirty and dusty as one would expect from a door that never saw an ounce of use. In fact, the reason that they had chosen to use the hazardous waste storage unit as an office was that none of the other employees particularly cared for paperwork. In their opinion, it may as well have been hazardous waste.

"I am indeed aware of your line of work, should one be liberal enough to call it as such. However, I am in need of a verbal description that I can include in my official report. I need to know how you perceive your assignment here."

"Well, we do a good job here." Aaron tried desperately to remember what the motto on the wall of the conference room so proudly proclaimed. They had had a manual at one point, but after a few weeks of operation, it had been lost among so many other things. "Our task is to predict world-ending events before they become an issue, and discover countermeasures and tactics to combat such an event."

"Straight out of the manual." The inspector muttered. Aaron breathed a sigh of relief. At least he had memorized it correctly. "Now, for the office."

Aaron held up his hands. "Are you sure that's needed?"

The inspector shook his head in disgust, reached for the door, and grasped the knob securely. As he pushed the door open, Aaron took a step back. If the inspector became hostile, he was going to need as much of a head start as he could get.

As the door swung open, a billowing cloud of dust swept outward, filling the hallway. The inspector stepped inside, and Aaron did his best to cough the dust out of his lungs before it made him sick. No telling what may have been in there since the last time they went inside.

When the inspector failed to reappear, Aaron risked a glance inside. It looked just as bad as he had assumed. Several shelves along the far wall were covered in piles of unfinished paperwork, much of which appeared to have been shredded to help build a large rodent nest under the desk. The only filing cabinet in the room was tipped on its side, and Aaron coughed at the sight of a pink tail vanishing into the expanse.

"This is your idea of keeping records?" The inspector shook his head, sending a shower of dust off his dirty blonde hair.

"Not in the slightest!" Aaron forced a laugh. "We have a techie kid who keeps track of all our recordkeeping on the computer. Much faster to find than having to sort through all those files. Plus you can access it from the comfort of home if you have any questions during your off-hours."

"You're using an easily hackable system to store top-secret governmental data."

"We…" Aaron fumbled for a response. "It's a pretty good system. Encrypted, all that kind of stuff."

"Right." The inspector shook his head. "So, this techie. What's his name?"

"Garmund." Aaron rubbed the back of his neck. "He's-"

"Garmund." The Inspector's eyebrows shot up into his forehead. "The hacker who was nearly executed a few years ago for hacking into the Pentagon?"

Aaron could only hold up his hands. "He was assigned here by General Herford. You'd have to ask him."

"Right." The inspector just shook his head. "Can I meet the rest of the team? I'd rather like to get his over with."

"They're-"

"You know, I think I'm done having you show me around." The inspector breezed back to the waiting room. "I think I'm going to take a look myself."

Aaron sank back against the wall. The moment that the inspector walked into the rear portion of the base, they were all toast. There simply wasn't anything more to it.

Slowly, knowing that he was heading to his own hanging, he followed the inspector. For a moment, he paused in the waiting room. It had been almost four years since anyone non-staff had set foot in the quaint, fifties-style room. Bright orange chairs sat on a blue pastel floor, the clashing colors nearly blinding the group every day they came to work. The receptionist's desk sat as the focal point for the room, despite being unused for years. The faded and slightly chipped paint seemed sad that now there would be no one around to ignore its presence.

Just behind the secretary's desk was a large set of steel double doors leading to the offices and emergency center. The inspector slammed his shoulder into the doors, grunting as they failed to budge an inch. He turned to glare at Aaron, and Aaron shrugged. No words were exchanged as he walked over to the lone painting hanging on the wall and pressed a small button concealed in the elaborate woodwork. The doors swung open with a whoosh, and the inspector breezed through.

Aaron followed closely, the doors nearly slamming shut on him as the pneumatic cylinders powered up. They now stood in a hallway that ran for about twenty feet. Three doors branched off to the right, leading to a number of offices, including Aaron's. A single door opened to the left. In a continuing streak of terrible fate, the door was wide open, allowing the inspector unimpeded access.

They stepped through the open door and into a small observation room. Rows of lights and buttons ran around the lower edge of a window that wrapped around three-quarters of the room. Through the glass, the Center of Operations could be seen, in all its glory.

The entire far wall, nearly thirty feet long, was covered in monitors that could be hooked up to any and every surveillance feed throughout the entire world. Covering the floor between the observation room and the monitors, a distance of about twenty feet, were dozens of consoles, computers, radios, and every other form of technological monitoring device imaginable.

Unfortunately, at that moment, the computer desks were being used to hold bags of potato chips, bottles of soda, crackers, and peanuts. Lawn chairs had been firmly wedged between the gaps in the desks, while the Monarchs baseball game roared on the main monitors.

The inspector crossed his arms and froze. Aaron couldn't bear to breathe as the man simply stood there, eyes gradually growing narrower and narrower.

"Can they hear us?" The inspector's voice was soft.

"No." Aaron stuttered. "The… This room is designed so that the commander of any active operation can express his frustration at how badly things are going without damaging the morale of his troops."

"I see." The inspector's voice was surprisingly calm. "Well, can you at least tell me that the entire team is here?"

Aaron began to rub the back of his neck a bit harder. "We're all here except one of us."

The inspector's groan was audible. "Is it too much to assume that he's sick with an incurable disease? Maybe the plague?"

Aaron opened his mouth, but was cut off as the lights in the room flashed red. A warning klaxon blared in the air, and the inspector snapped up straight. Aaron groaned as he saw his hacker, Garmund, smack the emergency button a few times for extra effect before grabbing a laptop off a nearby table.

"Should we be alarmed?" The inspector turned and started pacing. "This facility is tasked with emergencies, right? What's happening?"

Aaron put his head in his hands. "You'll find out in a minute. Something tells me that you won't be surprised."

The inspector frowned, but walked up to the window, clearly confused. Aaron was ninety percent sure he knew what was happening, but it took a few moments of watching the television monitors before he confirmed his suspicions.

The score was tied, 6-6, in the bottom of the ninth. The Monarchs were batting, bases loaded, two outs. Lloyd Bergil, the hot new rookie, was up to bat. The pitcher wound up, letting the ball fly. Instantly, the speed of the ball appeared on a screen in the lower left-hand corner of the wall. It sailed straight past Bergil, landing a perfect strike. The next pitch was the same, leaving only one possibility. Aaron held his breath as the pitcher wound up for, quite possibly, the final time.

With a crack that was amplified a hundred times by the massive speakers set in the floor of the room, the baseball was launched into the sky. It was long… But even then, Aaron could tell that it wasn't enough. It was going to come down in the middle of the outfield, get caught, and send the game into overtime. Traditionally, the Monarchs did terrible in overtime, which meant that if the ball came down, it was game over.

With a pop, the ball seemed to gain a new life midair. With the extra push, it sailed over the edge of the park, splashing firmly into a large fountain just in front of the cheap, student-section seats. The stadium exploded as the victory lap began. Monarchs win, 10-6!

Aaron let out a loud whoop and leapt back from the window, thrusting his fist into the air. In the control room, the group exploded. He saw popcorn go flying, but that was fairly commonplace. Who cared if they had to do a bit of cleaning afterward? It was a win!

"That's what I'm-"

His voice faded as he once again noticed the inspector standing there, eyebrows raised. There was a long pause before the inspector spoke again.

"You were wrong. That quite surprised me."

Aaron ran his hand through his hair. "Not a good thing?"

"That's the first sensible thing I've heard come out of your mouth." The inspector let out a long breath. "You want me to be frank with you?"

"Please do."

"Very well." The inspector simply shrugged. "As I'm sure you know by now, the only reason any of you have this building here is that you can't be fired. General Herford, for whatever reason, thinks that you deserve a second chance. I'm here to tell you that General Herford's power is beginning to diminish. He isn't going to be able to protect you much longer, and when his power fails, this little hideout of yours is going to be handed to someone else."

Aaron felt the room grow warm around him. "What happens to us, then?" He glanced down at the ground. "Where do we go?"

The inspector shrugged. "You, I suspect, will wind up on the side of the street in a box somewhere. The rest of these nutjobs will likely be placed in federal prisons or executed, depending on how much government data they've leaked during their stay here."

Aaron let out a breath. "Is there anything we can do?"

The inspector barked a laugh. "The only thing that comes to mind would be actually doing your job. Prevent the end of the world. Something like that."

Aaron paused. "Any ideas how to do that?"

The inspector simply snorted softly and ignored the question. "You have two weeks before my report makes it all the way through the system. At that time, you'll be subjected to a more formal investigation, led by the new General. He'll be the one that will make the final call on your fate."

Aaron paused, trying to remember what he had read in the news earlier that week. "Burchard, right?"

"Birch, but you're close." The inspector turned to leave. "Oh, in case you want to plead your case, here's my card. I'd honestly be interested to see what you come up with to grovel about."

Aaron took the thin slip of cardstock. "Thanks." The word came mindlessly from his lips, as he tried to comprehend the calamity falling down on them.

"You have an odd sense of thanks." The inspector chuckled, turned, and stalked away, vanishing through the facility.

Aaron glanced down at the card. Inspector Birch. Imagine that, he was related to the new general. Probably how he had gotten the position in the first place.

Granted, Aaron couldn't really complain about that. The only reason he had landed a job in the Apocalypse Prevention Department was that his Uncle Bruce was a general in the army as well. After dropping out of college to follow a failed art career, Aaron had wound up on a street corner in a cardboard box. His uncle had given him a complementary position in the military, only to realize quickly that Aaron simply wasn't cut out for the life of a soldier. A few months later, Aaron had found himself leading the worst division in the United States military. Now, though, it looked like he wouldn't even have that for long.

"Hey, man, we won!" Garmund opened the door to the control room and stepped inside. His clean-shaven face split in two with the size of his grin, and he held up a cheese-covered hand. "Pound it!"

Aaron took a deep breath, forced a grin, and held up his fist.

Garmund paused, his grin slowly vanishing. "Something really bad just happened, didn't it?"

"I sure as shooting hope not." Bertha stepped around Garmund, eyes flashing. Her hair exploded from her scalp in every direction, and in the red lighting, she looked as if she could have been the devil incarnate. Or at least one of the cartoon devils on TV. "Where in the wide world of sports were you? You missed Jasper's shot. Blast, that kid's an incredible sniper. You show me one other person in the military who can hit a moving baseball while…"

Her voice trailed off, and her eyes narrowed. "What's going on, Aaron? Spill it."

Aaron ran his hands through his hair, feeling the greasy locks twitching against his eyelids. "Garmund, get those alarms shut off. Bertha, I want the conference room cleaned up in half an hour. Jasper should be back from the game by then. We need to figure some things out."

"If you think I'm going to touch that room with anything resembling a sponge, you've got another thing coming." Bertha fixed him with a gaze.

"I'm not in the mood to deal with this." Aaron crossed his arms. "You get paid tomorrow afternoon. If the conference room isn't shining by the time we get together in half an hour, I'm delaying your wages until next pay period. You don't get any less, you just don't get it as quickly."

Bertha's eyes narrowed. "That's how you want to do things? Really?"

She put two fingers up to her eyes, then turned them around to point at Aaron's. After a moment, she flashed him a smile and walked past him, brushing up against Garmund as she did so. He glanced at her, and she wagged her hips at him for a brief moment before vanishing through the doorway. Garmund glanced at Aaron uncomfortably before walking over to a nearby computer. He began typing in strings of code, and the alarms fell silent.

After a few moments of thought, Aaron walked out of the command room and made his way to his office. Slowly, he cracked the door open and stepped inside. It was his one true sanctuary, the one place that he could truly get away from it all.

It was a mess, that was for certain. The desk that took up half the room was covered in folders containing who-knew-what types of information that he didn't care about. The shelves that ran around the room were covered in action figures, many of which came from childhood television shows. All that said, it was *his* mess. Not an ounce of clutter came from anyone else in the facility.

      He sat down in his chair, feeling the cushion beneath him strain to hold up his weight. After a moment of staring at his desk, he spun the chair slowly, watching the memorabilia turn around him. His desk rotated out of his sight, and the portrait of his uncle came into view. He had originally put it up to remind him of the greatness he could aspire to, the heights he could rise to. A large part of him wondered just how disappointed the general truly was in him. The portrait spun out of view, and with it, so did all hope of ever becoming something more in life. All he could do now was give the rest of the team a bit of advanced warning.

CHAPTER 2

"As soon as you're done getting the hay into the barn, I want you to start mucking out the sheep pens." Robert Ferguson gestured towards the low, tin-sided shelter that housed dozens of what had to be the stupidest farm animals on the planet. "If you manage to finish before five o'clock, start pulling the engine out of the old tractor. Sound good?"

Harold simply nodded, knowing that it would be futile to say a single word to the aging farmer. Robert stalked away, probably to chop wood, leaving Harold to his duties. After a moment, Harold turned to the massive hay trailer.

The trailer was nearly fifty feet long, twenty feet wide, and covered in square hay bales. It wasn't a lot of work, really, when an entire team worked together to get the job done. Shoot, it wasn't that big of a job to do if only two people were working together. By yourself, though, chucking hay bales wasn't exactly the most exciting job on the farm.

There was nothing to be done about it, though. Harold had taken the job, fair and square, and he needed the money. Working for Old Man Ferguson was the highest-paying job in the county, and the fact that he had managed to impress the man enough to get hired was, frankly, a miracle.

Slowly, Harold climbed up on top of the hay trailer and grabbed ahold of the nearest hay bale. With a mighty heave, he sent it flying away, down to the ground about ten feet away. His muscles, hardened from years of working in the sun, rippled as he worked. Too bad Robert didn't have any daughters to watch him work.

Harold chuckled at the thought. If Robert had ever been nice enough to someone to get married and have children, that time had long since passed. He was known for being nasty, hard, and cranky. Harold didn't mind him, per se. He just thought that the man had unreasonable expectations for how much could be done in a day.

Slowly, painstakingly, Harold continued to toss the bales off the back of the trailer and onto the ground. After he had thrown about thirty of them, he paused for a breath. There were still over a hundred left on the trailer, but he supposed that he should probably haul the ones on the ground into the barn. No sense in allowing Robert to catch him letting hay touch the dirt.

"Hey!" Robert's voice drifted around the barn as he hobbled into view. "What in tarnation do you think you're doing?"

Harold wiped his brow. "Chucking hay. You tell me how I'm supposed to get it off this trailer without letting it touch the ground, and I'll happily do it."

"You…" Robert sputtered for a moment before shaking his head. "If that hay gets left on the ground, it'll start to mold."

"I'm aware." Harold leapt from the back of the trailer, landing a few feet in front of the man. "However, I'm also aware that I'm not twenty feet tall, which means that I can't reach the top level of the trailer from the ground. They won't be on the ground for long."

Robert humphed. "See that they aren't."

Harold nodded and picked up the nearest bale of hay. He turned towards the barn, but stopped short. In the middle of barn, directly behind the back of an old tractor, the ground seemed to be bulging upward. Harold frowned as it pushed even higher, visibly pushing up out of the dirt floor.

"Robert?" Harold raised an eyebrow and turned towards the old farmer. "You don't have any excessively large gophers out here, do you?"

"Now why the…" Robert stopped short as he finally saw what Harold was looking at. Harold risked a glance at the old, wrinkled farmer, and was more than slightly surprised to see the man turning white. To his knowledge, he had never seen anything rattle the old codger.

"I take it you have an idea what this is?" Harold raised an eyebrow. "I'm kind of in the dark here."

"It can't be." Robert started walking toward the bulge. "Amelia?"

"Amelia?" Harold frowned. "Who's that?"

Robert paid him no attention, instead simply walking straight for the growing dirt mound. He stopped a few feet away, visibly trembling. Harold dropped the hay bale he was holding and slowly stepped to the side of the barn, where he took hold of a rather large pitchfork. No sense in being unprepared.

A moment passed while the dirt continued to build, now forming a pile nearly four feet high. Harold held his breath, hardly daring to breathe.

With a blast of dirt, an arm broke through the surface of the pile. From the little that Harold could see, it was mostly skin and bone, dried and rotted by the conditions of southwest Kansas. At least one of the fingers was missing, and he could see cracks in the skin where dried muscle tissue showed through.

A moment later, a second arm appeared, hands grasping for anything it could reach. Both hands clutched at the dirt, pulling *something* up and out of the soil. Even though Harold was expecting it, he still nearly screamed as the head appeared, a dried, pallid husk whose skin seemed shrink-wrapped to the skull. The eye sockets were simply filled with dirt, no life left in them.

After a few moments, the creature was completely out of its grave. For a few moments, it simply stood there, a few feet away from Robert. It wore a pale, rotted red dress that almost seemed pretty on it. Its head twisted back and forth, jaw working. Robert dropped to his knees in front of it, tears running down his face.

"You came back to me." He gasped. "After all these years, hoping, praying, wishing. You came back! So much has happened." He sucked in a deep breath. "Don't worry, I haven't been with any other woman. You can check the house for certain. Here, I'll have to show you the farm, it's been such a long-"

The creature, presumably the corpse of Amelia, lunged forward and snapped its jaws down on Robert's shoulder. Robert screamed and fell backward, blood spurting. The zombie bent down, bit into his neck, and started feasting.

Harold's jaw dropped at the sight. For that long moment, he simply found himself unable to move. What was he seeing? What was this girl? A zombie? Something else entirely? Was it going to come after him next? Was there any way to kill it before that happened?

Something tugged at his leg, and Harold glanced down. In an instant, he noticed an equally rotted corpse, this one a teenager, trying to chew through his jeans. Without thinking, he let out a yelp, kicked the corpse as hard as he could, and turned to run.

Two more corpses, both of them probably in their teens, stumbled towards him around the side of the barn. He brought up his pitchfork, realized the odds of killing something already long-dead, and jumped for the hay trailer. His hands caught on the metal sides, and he pulled himself upward, clawing his way higher and higher onto the stacks of bales.

When he reached the top, he risked a glance down. The corpse of Amelia had joined the other three, giving him four obstacles between himself and the barn. Unfortunately, his truck was on the opposite side of the building, which created another problem entirely.

Slowly, he started to breathe. The zombies weren't trying to climb the hay bales, so that was something. Their empty eye sockets simply stared up at him, watching and waiting for him to try to run. Harold took a deep breath and prepared himself. This was going to take some guts.

He bent down to jump, feeling an odd sense of excitement spring through his system. Only a few days earlier, one of the nerds at school had been going on and on about how he was ready for the zombie apocalypse. Well, now, he might actually get a chance to live that dream out.

A thought struck him a moment before he jumped. He was standing on a hay trailer with dozens of hundred-pound hay bales. Without a second thought, he picked up the closest bale, did his best to judge the distance, and threw it down at Amelia. She was crushed without a second thought, and he smiled. A few moments later, the rest of the undead family was gone, and he was happily climbing down to the ground. A few limbs twitched under the bales, but it was clear that nothing was getting up again. That, at least, was something positive.

Something moved in the door to the barn, and he groaned. Robert had probably reanimated as a zombie, hadn't he? Sure enough, Robert came stumbling from the barn, his walk uncertain, throat missing. Harold took a deep breath and charged around the side of the barn, running as fast as he could towards his truck. Even if there *was* only one, he didn't want to slip up and get eaten through some sort of stupid accident.

As he rounded the corner of the barn, truck in view, he realized that there was far from only one. Though they weren't human corpses, dozens of dogs were stumbling out of a tree row off to his left. Their fur was matted against their sides, caked with dirt and mud. Several of them appeared to be missing limbs, but it didn't seem to be slowing their progress. Their empty skulls swiveled in his direction, and they began to move faster, doing an odd sort of hopping that would have looked comical had they not been trying to eat him.

Harold just shook his head as he put on a burst of speed. He reached the truck a moment before the dogs, threw the door open, and leapt inside. The door slammed behind him, a handy perk of having an ancient vehicle missing a number of its parts.

Slowly, he took a deep breath, shuddering at the sound of the rotting claws scratching at his truck. He started the vehicle up, hoping that the noise might drive them away, but to no avail. After several long moments, he simply put the truck in drive and pressed down on the gas pedal.

It took a few moments to get turned around in the narrow driveway, but once he did, he speed away from the farm as quickly as he could. Dust billowed behind him, obscuring the buildings, and he puffed out his cheeks.

Well, that was one wave of zombies survived. It was a short drive back to his hometown of Lambspoint, where hopefully he could get some answers. His only question was whether the same thing was happening there, if things were better… Or if they were far worse.

CHAPTER 3

"So they're trying to shut us down." Bertha crossed her arms and leaned back in her chair. "What gives them the right?"

Aaron ran his finger along the edge of the glossily clean conference table. "They aren't just *trying* to shut us down, they're going to succeed. And I mean, we work for them, so they *do* have the right to do with us what they want."

"I say we fight it." Jasper slammed his hand onto the tabletop. The sharp movement nearly caused his beanie to fall from his head, and he frowned. "If they want to shut us down, it's because we're close to something. All we have to do is figure out what it is, then nail them to the wall with it."

"I can fire up my search algorithms again." Garmund held up his hands and glanced at Aaron. "I got some pretty good dirt the last time we used them. If I narrow the parameters a bit-"

"You think the whole world can just be hacked." Jasper crossed his arms and raised an eyebrow. "The world is *real,* not just some web of cyber data. I've seen what the government can do with the wrong tools, and that kind of stuff, you're not going to find on any computer. If we're going to dig up some dirt, we need to do it ourselves."

Garmund frowned. "I'm on your side. You realize that, right?"

"Look, this isn't getting us anywhere." Frank, the security guard, spoke up for the first time that meeting. Aaron turned his direction, thankful for the input. Frank rarely spoke, but when he did, it usually came from years of experience doing nearly everything under the sun. "We need to find a solution to the problem, and fast."

"Well, that's all fine and dandy." Bertha flashed her eyes at Frank. "What do you propose we do? Hacking their systems isn't going to give us anything we don't already have, and attacking their headquarters probably isn't going to secure our jobs."

Frank nodded, wrinkles bobbing on his face. "Exactly my point. If we exhibit any form of aggressive behavior, I suspect that the results won't be favorable. Now, I believe that when Mr. Birch came here, he gave us one possibility of keeping our jobs."

Aaron barked a laugh. "He said that to save our jobs, we would have to *do* our jobs. Save the world. Well, I don't exactly see any scenario that really fits our bill, do you? I mean, that was kind of the point when we were formed. We wouldn't be able to do anything."

"Then perhaps we need to look harder." Frank pressed. "Did you read the newspaper this morning?"

Aaron shook his head. "I was too busy getting snacks for the Monarchs game."

Frank turned to the rest of the team. "Any of you?"

A round of head shakes went around the table, and Frank sighed. "Alright, fine. Here's the deal. Dr. Incacheck was reportedly seen in western Kansas late last night. The witness said that he was driving a large white van with tinted windows that was filled with scientific equipment. That means-"

"That means we need to run the other way as quickly as possible." Garmund stood up and held up his hands. "That guy only brings trouble."

"Not *that* Incacheck." Frank waved his hand. "The younger Incacheck."

A sigh of relief went around the table. Idly, Aaron couldn't understand why two scientists with plans to end the world had the same name. It made matters more than slightly confusing for everyone on the planet who was trying to figure out who to be afraid of. Couldn't one of them have chosen a different name or something?

"Let's see here." Garmund frowned. "Young Incacheck specializes in biological warfare, right?"

"Yes." Frank nodded. "The article speculated that he's going to be using one of the small towns out there for some sort of experiment. Wipe one of them off the map, and no one really knows the difference. It probably wouldn't even be printed in most of the major papers."

"Then what are you suggesting?" Aaron frowned. "We head out to western Kansas to try and confront this guy before he destroys something? Call that 'saving the world?'"

"Well, it would be better than sitting here all day talking." Garmund shrugged. "Besides, it's probably just a false alarm anyway. With small towns being what they are, it would be easy enough for us to type up a few reports, create some false interviews, come up with a good world-ending event that we manage to prevent at the last moment."

"Sounds good to me." Bertha crossed her arms. "Minimal work for maximum outcome. I knew there was a reason I liked this computer geek."

Garmund scooted his chair a few inches away from Bertha, who looked like she was leaning towards him. Jasper put his hands on the arms of his chair and forced himself up.

"Well, if we're going to do this, we're going to need some pretty convincing weaponry to pull it off." The weapons expert frowned at Garmund. "We can create all the fake news that we want, but we're going to actually need to *show* that something happened. What say we blow up a barn or two while we're out there? Maybe an abandoned warehouse?"

"It would help substantiate the idea that we're actually fighting something." Aaron shrugged. "Load up the van with whatever you want. Just nothing nuclear-powered, okay? The last time-"

"Yeah, yeah, yeah." Jasper huffed. "I get the picture."

He walked out of the room, presumably heading towards his weapons locker, and Aaron turned to

Garmund. "Alright, I need you to find a good small town we can wreck."

"On it." Garmund pulled up his laptop and started typing on the keys. "What are we looking for?"

Aaron paused. "We need something small, less than two hundred people. No newspaper with a wider circulation than the city limits and less than five percent of the population registered on any sort of social media. Preferably with a number of abandoned buildings from long-past glory days, and-"

"I think I have it." Garmund slid the laptop across the table. "It's a small town called Bethel. Located about fifty miles south of Garden City, no local school district, most of the residents are fifty and older, almost no social media accounts, plenty of old buildings. We should be able to fake some pictures of Dr. Incacheck, drum up some interviews, the whole kit and caboodle!"

Frank held up a hand. "You know, I was actually going to suggest that we try and capture Dr. Incacheck. He *has* killed thousands of people through his research, and probably *will* destroy a city or two while he's out there. If we blow up a city only to find that he was *also* blowing up a city at the exact same time, it's not going to look too good for us."

Aaron let out a long breath. It wasn't that Frank was *wrong*, but... "We'll play it by ear. If it happens, we're not any more toast than we are now. In any event, like Garmund said, there's a slim chance that he actually *is* out there. There are thousands of sightings of both doctors per day. He could be anywhere in the world. I think we're safe."

Bertha held up a hand, as if still in elementary school. "Besides, we're trying *not* to do our job? Get with the program."

Frank held up his hands in mock surrender. "Alright, do as you please."

"You're coming with us." Aaron raised his eyebrows. "Someone has to watch the cameras."

"I guess." Frank forced himself to his feet. "I'll see you in the van. Let me grab some snacks for the road."

"We roll out in three hours." Aaron held up his hand. "Be ready by then!"

Now, it was only Bertha and Aaron left in the room. Bertha cocked an eyebrow at him and leaned forward. "Any work for me?"

"You'll be driving one of the vans." Aaron shrugged. "Anything more you're wanting to do?"

"Not on your life." Bertha stood up and sauntered out of the room. Aaron followed her for a moment, wondering again and again why in the world she had been picked up by the government in the first place. The rest of them at least had *some* sort of viable reason why they weren't simply fired or executed.

While the rest of the team went to work, Aaron walked back to his office. As the unofficial spokesperson for the team, he knew that it would come down to him to prepare the official statement to give to inspector Birch after it was all said and done. It was as good a time as any to start working on the final report then and there.

CHAPTER 4

Harold tore through the first stop sign of the town, not because he was running from the zombies, but because everyone did. Lambspoint only had a few hundred residents, all of whom drove distinctly different vehicles. If you saw one of them on the road, you probably knew where they were heading, so there was no use for things like turn signals or stop signs.

As it was, he was so focused on getting home that he nearly rammed into the side of the sheriff's car as the dusty white vehicle pulled out of the Home and Deli parking lot. The lights flickered for a brief moment, and Harold pulled the vehicle to a stop. He rolled down his window, and the sheriff pulled up next to him.

"Going somewhere?" Bernard Thompson, the county sheriff, chuckled as he rolled down his passenger window, allowing the two to talk. "You're usually one of the more responsible drivers in town."

"Sorry about that." Harold shook his head. "Today… Today's a little weird."

"Weird how?" Bernard narrowed his eyes. "You didn't run into one of those gangs from the city, did you?"

"No." Harold shook his head. "No, they're staying put, for now. Can I ask a question?"

"Fire away."

"Have there been any strange reports today?" Harold scratched his forehead. "Coming specifically from the graveyard or the coroner's office?"

"Old Marge was carrying on about the dead rising from their graves." Bernard shrugged. "So, nothing new. Besides, even if it *wasn't* normal for her, no one would be listening anyway. Everyone's over at the exhibit."

"Exhibit?" Harold frowned for a moment before nodding. "Oh, that's today, isn't it? I'd forgotten that was coming to town."

"A bit of the Smithsonian, right in our backyards." Bernard chuckled. "It's down at the city park, you should really go check it out."

"I will." Harold nodded before coming back to the matter at hand. "Wait. You said that Old Marge was talking about the dead coming back to life?"

"Yeah." Bernard frowned. "You know something?"

Harold frowned before nodding. "I was out at Old Man Ferguson's farm. Did he used to have a family?"

Bernard nodded in confusion. "I thought I was the only one old enough to remember his family. Well, me and Old Marge. They all died of smallpox when I was probably eight years old. How'd you find out about them? He doesn't like to talk about it much."

Harold shrugged. "Well, one of them came crawling up out of the barn floor. Three more came from somewhere else, tried to eat my leg off. They *did* manage to take a bite out of Ferguson. Oh, and a whole bunch of his old farm dogs came up out of an old hedge row, tried to take a piece out of me."

Bernard frowned. "You're a solid kid, and you don't look like you're on drugs. Old Man Ferguson's place, you said?"

Harold nodded. "I crushed a bunch of them under some hay bales and drove over some more, so even if the rest have wandered off, you'd still be able to find something."

Bernard nodded slowly. "It's only a ten-minute drive. Let me head out there, check some things out. Chances are good that Ferguson wasn't overly fond of things like caskets or going the full six feet, which means that if corpses *are* rising, they probably made their appearance there before they'll be able to break free out here. Get home, get inside, start telling everyone else to do the same. I'll get Deputy Monty to help."

"And I'm going to tell people that they're being hunted by zombies?" Harold cocked an eyebrow.

"No. You're going to tell them that an exceptionally large pack of wild dogs has been spotted a few miles south of town, heading our direction." Bernard sighed. "That should do the trick, at least for most people."

"On it." Harold shifted his car back into drive. "Be safe."

"I've survived gunfights in this town." Bernard chuckled. "A walking carcass isn't going to take me down."

Harold nodded, only to start coughing as a vehicle roared by, sending up a massive cloud of dust. He frowned as he realized that it was from out of town. At least, no one he knew drove a solid white van with heavily tinted windows.

Bernard sighed as the rampant van tore turned a corner. "I suppose I should also check out the stranger. Could be there's a connection. Ahh, at least something interesting is happening."

With that, Bernard flicked on the lights and took off. Harold chuckled, pulled away from the curb, and turned right at the intersection. His house was near the edge of town, which he had always enjoyed. It allowed them to keep several chicken cages in their backyard, along with the occasional goat. Their last goat had just died a few weeks earlier, though, leaving a mostly-abandoned expanse behind their home.

As he pulled up, he saw the door swinging shut. Curious, he frowned. His parents should have still been at work, and there was no one else who should have been going inside. The only possible other intruder was his stepsister, but she usually only came home late at night. Plus, he knew that if the Smithsonian exhibit had indeed arrived, she would be hard at work volunteering with the displays. There was nothing she loved more than history, that was for certain. Well, except for boys.

Carefully, Harold shut the car off and cracked the door open. When no snarls or moans reached his ears, he nodded and stepped out. If there were any corpses around, they were keeping quiet. Which only left whatever had just entered his home…

He walked up to his front door, being careful to step on the boards that didn't creak. It had become essential to know which were which, as his parents weren't exactly fond of him sneaking off in the night. Slowly, he grabbed the door handle and cracked it open. A distinct bump sounded from within, and he slipped his hand into his pocket, pulling out a small knife. It wasn't much, but it made him feel a bit better.

Hardly daring to breathe, he cracked the door open and peered inside. Nothing could be seen, though he could distinctly hear something moving around. It sounded like it was coming from the kitchen, and he slipped inside the house.

With a rush, the door to the kitchen blew open. He thrust his knife upward, ready to face whatever demons were pouring forth. A torn dress fluttered in his vision, and he took a step backward.

"Put that thing away!" Sharron, his stepsister, waved at the knife. "Are you trying to kill me?"

"I was trying to kill *something*." Harold muttered, folded the knife, and stuck it back in his pocket. "What in the world are you doing here?"

"I was helping down at the exhibit and tore my dress." Sharron muttered and looked down at the shredded red cloth. "Your mom keeps sewing equipment in the kitchen, I came here to get it fixed up."

Harold nodded and ran his hand through his hair. He almost reminded her that his mom was *technically* her mom as well, since the adoption had legally gone through, *but...* "Well, it's probably better you're here anyway. I want you to lock all the doors and start boarding up the windows. Make sure nothing can get inside."

Sharron frowned. "Why? A group of bandits coming into town?"

"Something like that." Harold muttered. Bandits? Did she think they lived in the wild west or something? "There's a pack of wild dogs that was seen a few miles south of here. Seems they enjoy attacking people, and they're heading this way. I'm heading out to spread the news."

"You're going to go out and face this danger while I hide in the house like a little girl?" Sharron cocked an eyebrow.

"No, I'm going to grab a shotgun and start going door to door telling everyone else to hide, and then I'm going to join you." Harold shrugged. "It's as simple as that."

Sharron bit her lip. "Alright, then. Be safe."

"You too." Harold nodded, knowing that she wouldn't have batted an eye at his being devoured. "Like I said, make sure *nothing* gets inside."

Sharron narrowed her eyes, but nodded. Harold ran for the stairs, tearing to his parents' bedroom as quickly as he could. Once inside, he ran for their closet, where his stepfather's gun closet was. It took a matter of seconds to grab the large, 12-gauge shotgun from the racks. A few moments later, he grabbed a small pistol that he stuck in his belt and slung a hunting rifle over his back. No sense in being unprepared.

As he walked out the front door, Sharron crossed her arms and looked at him, and he just grinned back. There was no sense trying to explain the undead to her before she saw one for herself. She was a very "show-me" person, trying to reason would get him nowhere. Besides, he was pretty certain that it wouldn't be much longer before the streets were flooded with the undead.

He walked down the sidewalk to his car, feeling an odd sense of protection coming from the shotgun. It was nice, knowing that even if he couldn't kill the creatures, he could at least blow their limbs off them.

He had just put his hand on the door handle when a loud explosion echoed from the center of town. He spun that way to see a large cloud of black smoke coming from the approximate location of the city park. A moment later, the sheriff's car tore around the bend, heading straight towards Harold's house. Harold raised an eyebrow as Bernard screeched to halt in front of his driveway. The aging head poked out of the driver's window, panic in his eyes.

"You know how I said it would be awhile?"

Harold nodded. "Yeah?"

"Well, the cemetery just overflowed."

Harold felt a flash of horror. "The cemetery is right next to the city park, where the exhibit is."

"Yep. And one of those idiots down there got the idea to try to use a World War Two era bomb to blow the things up." Bernard shrugged. "Let's just say that there's going to be a lot more dead rising before too much longer."

"What are you suggesting?" Harold crossed his arms.

"We've got to get out of here!" Bernard waved his hands. "I saw at least a hundred bodies crawling over the church fence. This town is going to be overrun in a matter of minutes. Get whoever you're with and let's go. Maybe they'll believe two witnesses once we get to Garden City, send some police reinforcements back with us."

Harold shook his head. "What about everyone here? We're just going to leave them?"

"You want to fight all that?" Bernard pointed backward. Harold glanced that way to see dozens of corpses stumbling around the corner, heading straight for them. Several of the leaders broke into a run, and Harold brought up his gun.

"Just get inside!" Bernard waved at the door. "Now! Everyone else will be safe enough if they're smart."

Harold hesitated for a moment, then ran for the side door, wrenched it open, and dove inside. The moment the door was shut, tires squealed, and they were off. Harold did his best to hold his guns on his lap as they passed the edge of town. He had told Sharron to keep the doors shut. Hopefully, she actually would. The zombies didn't seem overly intelligent, which meant that she was *probably* safe. His parents, specifically his stepdad, would *kill* him if she wound up dying.

"What happened with the stranger?" Harold sighed and tried to get the guns situated on his lap better. "Any leads?"

"No idea." Bernard shrugged. "He made it to the exhibit, got out for a few seconds, just to get back in his van as soon as the graves started breaking open. He hadn't moved when I left."

"Maybe he's some sort of zombiekiller." Harold chuckled. "At least we can hope."

"That we-"

Bernard was cut off as the car slammed into *something*. Harold didn't even have a moment to be surprised before the airbag blew outward, slamming into his face. His head was blown backward into the seat, and he groaned at the acidic taste of blood in his mouth. His ears rang like sirens, and the world seemed tilted.

Slowly, his vision swam back into focus. Beside him, Bernard was slumped over the steering wheel, just behind a very cracked windshield. The old man's airbag was nowhere to be seen, it simply hadn't deployed. Cuts covered the man's face, giving no illusions that he was dead. Nevertheless, Harold reached over and grabbed him, feeling for a pulse. When he couldn't feel anything, he paused. He had known Bernard for years, ever since he was born. The thought that a faulty airbag had managed to do in the wiry old man was sobering.

A thought struck him a moment later, and he scrambled to undo his seatbelt as fast as he could. He fingers, slick with sweat, skimmed over the button to release the clasp, and he swore. He didn't know if he would come back as a zombie, but...

Beside him, Bernard began to stir. Harold screamed, smashed his hand into the buckle, feeling the satisfactory click beneath his palm. With a rush, he dove to the side, throwing the car door open as quickly as he could. His arm got caught in the belt as he fell to the ground, and he scrambled frantically to escape. When his arm finally *did* come free, it was one of the most exhilarating feelings he had ever experienced.

He didn't slow down until he was well over fifty feet away from the vehicle. Slowly, he forced himself to his feet, swinging the rifle over his shoulder as he did so. He gripped the shotgun with a death hold, never letting its sights waver. One foot went in front of the other, and he began to move back towards the vehicle.

Inside, Bernard thrashed against the restraints, failing to move so much as an inch closer to Harold. His arms stretched out, clawing at the air, and his jaw worked in an odd snapping motion, as he if was trying to take a bite out of his friend. When Harold realized that there simply wasn't any way that Bernard was going to get to him, he sighed, frowned, and aimed the gun. It just… It wasn't right to let such an honorable man die like that.

The first blast went through the zombie's chest, showering the inside of the cab in blood but failing to slow down the zombie's headlong sprawl so much as one bit. Curious, Harold adjusted his aim.

The next blast went straight to the head, and Bernard fell still. Harold grimaced at the sight. He was glad to have stopped the monster, but… That had been *Bernard!* The guy who gave everything for his town. The guy who would show up while you were painting your house and lend a hand. The guy who was always in church, just a few rows back. The guy who would only arrest or fine you if you were from out of town or if he hadn't had his morning coffee yet.

Slowly, Harold shook his head. After a moment of silence, Harold walked to the front of the car. Interestingly, it seemed as if the vehicle had simply run into thin air. There wasn't even a pothole in the road.

Harold walked in front of the car, an odd tingling feeling rising on the back of his neck. It felt like an old tube television set, the feel of more static electricity than anything had a right to emit. He turned around, facing the road that led away from Lambspoint and towards Garden City. Carefully, he took a step forward.

An electric jolt like a thousand lightning bolts shot through his system, and he was flung backward onto the crushed hood of the vehicle. He shook his head and stood back up, mind whirling. A force field? Could... Could that even be real?

Curious, he walked to the side of the road and started walking forward. If the force field only covered the roads, he could still escape the city on foot.

It was to no avail, though, as he was once again launched backward, this time landing flat on his back in the ditch. After taking a deep breath, he forced himself to his feet and faced the town. Maybe the mysterious wall didn't go all the way around the town, maybe there was another way out. Then again, there was a strong chance that there wasn't. The only surefire way to survive was to kill everything dead that was trying to come back to life again.

One foot went in front of the other, and he started walking back towards town. He would go to his house, talk through the situation with Sharron, and go from there. The best chance they had was to get to the school building, chances were good that other survivors would try to meet there. It was the most fortified building in the area, and it was the center of most town social activities. If they only found the dead inhabiting the halls, well... There was only one solution.

CHAPTER 5

"I hate hotel rooms." Bertha swept through the chipped doorway and flopped onto the puke-green bedspread. "They just reek. I mean, who knows what went on here? It's disgusting."

"It's what we have to deal with." Aaron shrugged and sat down on the opposite bed. "Garmund? This going to work?"

"It should." Garmund stood up from where he was inspecting the phone lines. "The connection looks bad on the outside, but with a bit of splicing I should be into the network easily enough."

"Good." Aaron nodded. "Frank? You good to go in the security department?"

"You tell me." Frank muttered as he stumbled into the room, lugging a larger suitcase than any of the rest of them. "In the old days, a security guard sat on the roof of the building with a sniper rifle. Now we have bird-cameras-"

"Drones."

"Whatever. *Drones*, computer monitors, it just feels like all I ever do is sit in a room and eat." Frank tossed the suitcase on the nearest table, knocking several lamps to the floor, and flipped the latch. Instantly, computer screens popped up out of the fake leather. A keyboard slid out of the front, and a rack of drones rose out of the back. He plopped into a chair, pulled out a bag of chips, and looked at them. "What?"

"Nothing." Bertha shrugged. "We just think you're really good at your job."

Frank turned to glare at Bertha, then spun back to his screens. "Does this thing have an active newsfeed?"

"Not at the moment, but it would be easy enough to install." Garmund stepped up to the portable surveillance device. "Give me three seconds. What are you looking for?"

"Any and all local online news. And the larger papers. The ones from New York and Washington. Oh, and anything mentioning Incacheck."

Garmund nodded through it all. A moment later, one of the screens changed to a flickering view of news from across the world. Garmund swept out his hand, and Frank nodded.

"Good enough. When do we start?"

"You can launch those drones now." Aaron shrugged. When nothing happened, he pointed at the keyboard. "The big red button in the corner."

"You want me to press that?" Frank's eyes narrowed. "I thought you were never supposed to press big red buttons. That's why they're red."

Jasper shook his head. "Big red buttons are *made* to be pushed. The actual critical systems are always triggered by a much smaller, usually difficult-to-find button."

"In that case…" Frank muttered and pressed the button. The drones began to launch in sequence, shooting through the room and nearly taking Garmund's head off. As the last one exited the room, a muffled boom made the windows shudder.

Frank frowned. "Did one of the cameras just explode?"

"Drones." Jasper corrected. "And no. If one of those things was to explode, we'd feel it. Their cores *should* create a blast radius of about three feet, with a solid concussion for another hundred feet or so."

"Please believe me when I say that I don't need those details." Aaron forced himself to his feet and stepped out the door. "I wonder what it could have been, then?"

In the distance, barely visible on the western horizon, a small cloud of smoke could be seen rising into the sky. Aaron frowned and nodded back at Frank. "Can we track that?"

"What are you talking about?" Frank frowned. "You track deer, not explosions."

Aaron walked back inside the room. "Can you send one of those drones to see what's going on over there? If it's something major, we could use it in our report."

"Fine. On it." Frank frowned as he looked at the keyboard. Garmund reached over his shoulder and pressed several buttons. One of the screens changed as the drone swung away, and Frank just shook his head. "It's much easier when the cameras don't move."

"Well, you're going to need to figure this system out." Aaron waved at the team. "Start moving through the town, scoping things out. You all brought your badges, right?"

There was a round of head-nods, and Aaron crossed his arms. "Good. Find us some buildings to blow up, figure out who we can interview. Frank, I want you to get lots of footage that Garmund can add Dr. Incacheck's picture into. Ready? Break!"

With that, Aaron walked out of the room and started stalking across the parking lot. The sun was just starting to set, which meant that he had a few prime hours before people started to go to bed and become annoyed by his presence. The rest of the team followed, slowly spreading out. Well… Mostly spreading out. Bertha followed Garmund like a hound dog, to the poor programmer's dismay.

As the rest of the team filled out into the rest of the town, Aaron made his way into the hotel lobby. One thing he had learned while in the military was that you could question a person about something that never happened, talk to them about it later, and manage to convince them that it had, indeed, happened. The receptionist looked up at him, blew a bubble, and yawned.

"Somethin' the matter with your room?"

"No, the room is fine." Aaron sighed and pulled out his government badge. It *technically* didn't give him any extra rights, but the receptionist didn't need to know that. "Do you mind if I ask you some questions?"

"As long as they don't require me to reveal the identity of anyone who is staying or has stayed here, corporate information, or personal information, yes." The lady rolled her eyes upward. "At least that's what the manual says. We've only had a few guests here in the last month. I can't imagine why they keep this place up, anyway. The only people who stay the night are folks who break down on their way to Colorado and can't make it back into Garden City."

"Good." Aaron nodded, ignoring her tirade. "Have you heard of a Dr. Incacheck?"

"That guy who took over a small country in South America?" The receptionist cocked an eyebrow. "Claims to possess technology powerful enough to bend the entire world to his will?"

"No." Aaron let out a breath. "The other Incacheck. The younger one."

"Oh, the mad scientist." The receptionist nodded. "I've heard a few things. Not as much, mind you, but enough."

"Have you seen him recently?" Aaron shrugged. "He'd be driving a white van with heavily tinted windows. Probably wearing a brown hoodie, blue jeans, and sunglasses."

"Oh, he came through yesterday." The receptionist shrugged. "I mean, it was a blue hoodie, not a brown one. About six feet tall, clean shaven, has a scar on his cheek? License plate X-Y-B-three-zero-three. Iron-plated wheels. A mess of an arsenal in the back. Oh, and he went by the name Martin."

Aaron's eyebrows shot up. "That's oddly specific."

"I told you, we don't get many visitors." The lady shrugged. "He was in room twenty-three if you want to sweep it for chemical evidence. You government people do that, right? He had all sorts of lab equipment set up in there."

"You looked in on him?" Aaron thought that was a *bit* disturbing for a hotel receptionist, even if it *was* getting information.

"I look in on a lot of people." The lady shrugged and blew another bubble, popping it loudly. "Most people don't care. Some invite me in."

Aaron shook his head. He did *not* need to hear about what the woman did with her guests. "What did he do?"

"He didn't. He was too busy laughing maniacally." The lady shrugged. "You ask me, the guys tries too hard to be an evil genius. You have to just let those things come naturally."

"Thanks." Aaron nodded. "That's what we needed to know."

"You haven't even asked where he was going after that." The lady held up her hands. "You *are* trying to track this guy, right? Because if you are, you might want to go check out Lambspoint."

"Lambspoint?" Aaron chuckled. "What kind of a name is that?"

"It's a town about twenty miles west of here." The lady shrugged. "That's where this guy said he was heading. I asked why he didn't just drive there, and he told me because it was late and there wasn't a hotel in the city limits. He was kind of shifty when he said it, though. You ask me, he's up to somethin'."

Aaron let out a breath. He rather wasn't liking where the conversation was going. "That's what we need to know. Thanks for the information. Anything else?"

The lady twirled a strand of hair in her fingers. "If any of you get bored, the manager never comes around. That's information that a lot of my guests enjoy hearing."

Aaron shook his head and walked back out into the street. He took a deep breath, let out and jumped ten feet in the air as another explosion, this one *much* closer, shook the parking lot. He spun to see fire belch into the sky on the opposite side of the hotel. As he tore around the side of the building, he saw a building collapsing in a fiery death. He desperately hoped it had been abandoned, because the hapless gunner standing in front of it certainly gave no illusions about its fate.

"Jasper!" Aaron ran over. "I thought we weren't blowing up any buildings until *after* we finished reconnaissance."

"Don't blame me." Jasper muttered. "Frank flew one of those drones at my head. I barely managed to duck out of the way, the thing crashed into the front door of that place, and it exploded."

Aaron crossed his arms. "You said they only have an explosion radius of three feet."

"That was my *estimate*." Jasper shrugged. "I was a little off."

Aaron coughed as smoke from the explosion drifted his way. A car turned onto the street and cruised past the destruction before vanishing into the small town. "Who built those things?"

"I bought the drones from the government." Jasper shrugged and readjusted bis beanie. "Garmund and I beefed up their programming and power source, but-"

"Remind me to never let you overcharge something ever again." Aaron sighed. "In any event, we need to get back to the room. I have information for us. Information that completely changes the game."

CHAPTER 8

Harold took a deep breath as he jogged back towards the town. The herd of zombies was now scattered as the creatures wandered aimlessly, back and forth. He slowed down and crouched, trying not to draw any attention to himself.

All of the corpses that he could see looked more or less the same. They were old, weathered similarly to the zombies that he had seen out on the farm. No newly dead bodies, which was something to be thankful for. One of them swiveled in his direction and snapped its rotting jaw once before lurching down the road towards him.

Harold closed his eyes for a brief moment before lifting his rifle. He sighted down the barrel, lining up the shot perfectly. The creature moved so slowly, he couldn't understand how it was possible *not* to miss. He let out a soft breath and squeezed the trigger.

The zombie's head snapped backward, and its rotting forehead exploded. A sickening thud echoed through the silence in the space after the rifle shot, and Harold winced.

In a single motion, dozens of zombies across the area simultaneously turned and lurched in his direction, all emitting groans that could have woken the dead. It was unreal, seeing *that* many creatures all trying to kill him, even slowly. For a brief moment, he found himself unable to move in simple fear and awe.

The fear faded as the reality of the situation dawned on him. He brought up his gun again and fired a shot at the next closest zombie. The bullet tore through its neck, doing merely cosmetic damage. Harold swore and fired off three more shots, taking down two of the creatures but failing to stop the horde in its entirety.

By now, Harold counted at least thirty zombies zeroing in on his location. He began to walk backward and slung the rifle over his shoulder. He was in the process of switching to his shotgun when a hand came down on his shoulder.

Harold screamed and spun away as a zombie tried to bite down on his shoulder. He almost dropped his shotgun, turned, and ran. His home the last house on the row, less than a hundred feet away. Forget trying to shoot everything then and there. He would get inside, get to safety, and *then* he could start hunting the creatures.

The zombies slowly changed direction as he ran, like a slug trying to follow the motion of a rabbit. It was almost comical, in a way. If only there weren't *so* many of them. Harold reached the fence around their backyard and jumped over it in a single smooth motion, landing behind the wooden protection. Slowly, he turned and grinned at the shambling corpses still following him.

"And *that* is why I'm going to win." He mocked the creatures as they swarmed towards the fence. Slowly, he lifted up his shotgun and emptied the first barrel into the head of the closest monster. It fell, and he shot the second one, too. More continued to come, and he lowered his gun to reload. The first zombie piled up against the fence, and he smiled. It wasn't an *extraordinary* fence, but it was going to be strong enough to…

Without pausing, the zombie tore straight through the wood and continued stomping towards Harold. Harold's eyes went wide, and he turned to run yet again. More of the creatures began to crash through other parts of the backyard, and, for a moment, he turned towards the back door of his home.

Which was when he realized an inherent flaw in his plan. If the zombies were strong enough to tear through the fences, they were going to be strong enough to tear through the doors, too. Which meant that he needed to get inside without being seen. Without pausing, he turned and tore through the gate into the front yard. Several zombies on the far side of the street groaned and turned to moved towards him. One of them happened to be just behind his truck, and quite unhelpfully shoved it out of the way, popping one of the tires in the process.

Harold groaned and ran along the side of the house. A scraggly tree sat next to the porch, and with a burst of effort that would have made the track coach proud, he threw himself up into the thin branches. The wood emitted a series of cracks under his weight, but he didn't stay in the tree long enough for it to matter. With another groan, he tossed himself up onto the porch roof, out of reach of the creatures.

Below him, growls and moans echoed upward as the zombies lost interest and began to simply mill around again. It was just like on the farm. They could see him, but for whatever reason, saw no reason to try and climb up. Harold continued to frown down at them for a few moments, trying to think. He brought up his rifle and sighted in on the closest zombie, then shook his head. If his shots continued to attract attention, the zombies might wind up breaking through the door into the home anyway.

After several long moments, he sighed, then turned and used the butt of his shotgun to smash through the nearest window. He stepped through the broken glass into Sharron's room. She jumped up from where she lay on the bed, a frown on her face.

"Why in the world would you-"

"Take a glance out the window." Harold ignored her and walked to the door into the hallway. "Tell me what you think."

Sharron glanced through the shattered screen. Harold heard her scream, and he chuckled. He reached the kitchen a few moments later as her feet pounded on the stairs behind him. She began to sputter while he started reloading his weapons.

"What's going on?" Her voice was shrill. "What are those things?"

"Zombies." Harold shrugged. "I was *hoping* that things wouldn't get this bad, but…"

He proceeded to explain everything that had happened up to that moment. By the time he finished, Sharron swayed back and forth like a tree. She looked like she was ready to pass out, which wasn't helpful given the situation.

"Sharron." Harold waved a hand in front of her face. "We need to get going."

"You want to *what?*" Sharron snapped back to reality and looked at Harold like he had transformed into a goat. "Leave the house?"

"We're only safe in here as long as they don't see us." Harold nodded at the back door. A thump sounded as one of the creatures stumbled back and forth on the porch. "Those things are slow, but they're insanely strong. They'll be able to claw through doors, walls, and anything else we could put up. We're honestly probably better off running through the streets where we can at least move faster than them."

"And then what happens?" Sharron crossed her arms. "We shoot them, run out of bullets, and run until you run out of breath. Then they catch up with us and we die."

"If we can make it to the school, we'll be behind metal barriers." Harold crossed his arms. "We have to at least try."

"You can go, but I'm not getting myself killed." Sharron shook her head and turned away. "You'll have to go without me."

Harold's head dropped. "At least lock yourself in the storm shelter. If they get in the house, they'll have a harder time breaking through that door."

"You're going to leave me?" Her eyes filled with water. "You're actually going to-"

"I have to do something!" Harold threw his arms up. "Who knows how many people are out there without weapons, just trying to survive? If we can help them, we have to try."

A thump sounded on the front door, and Harold froze. Sharron crossed her arms.

"Good going. You attracted them with all your stupid yelling."

With a crack, the wall behind Sharron splintered as a zombie tore through the boards. Its decayed hand latched down on Sharron's arm, and she screamed and tried to pull away.

Harold brought up his gun and fired a shell into the monster's head. It exploded, and the creature collapsed. Behind it, he could see dozens of other zombies in the yard, turning in his direction.

"Come on, Sharron." Harold held out his hand. "We need to-"

Sharron shook her head. "Get away from me!"

"I just need to-"

"We're not safe anywhere!" Sharron turned and ran for the basement stairs. "Get away!"

Harold paused. He could follow her, but he knew that he wouldn't be able to convince her to come with him. As the front door was broken into splinters, he stepped through the opening into the living room.

"Hey, you!" He held up the gun. "Eat lead!"

The shot wound up hitting the zombie in the lower neck, shattering bones, but doing no permanent damage to the moving corpse. The second shell missed as well, striking the neck once more. Thankfully, *that* caused the head to fall from the shoulders, landing with a thud on the floor. The body gave several jerks before collapsing as well, landing firmly on the head.

Harold glanced back at the swarm of zombies that tore through the kitchen and roared through the home. He turned and ran out the front door, glancing back and forth. Thankfully, only a few zombies were in his immediate area, and he turned and ran towards the center of town, towards the school.

A scream echoed through the town as the last rays of the sun vanished, and he let out a long breath. This was going to be a long night, he could feel it. The only question was who would survive… and who would be eaten.

CHAPTER 7

"Well, that's that." Garmund crossed his arms. "I'm heading back to Kansas City." He closed his laptop, slid it into his pack, threw the pack on his shoulder, and stood up. "Who's with me?"

"Remind me how this is a bad thing?" Frank frowned. "We need to find Dr. Incacheck. We go to stage his appearance, we find out that he's only a few miles away, and we run. That doesn't make sense!"

"That about sums it up." Aaron clapped him on the shoulder. "Look at us. We're in no condition to fight someone like that. I mean, he just blew something up! Do we have that kind of firepower?"

"Technically, yes." Jasper held up a hand. "The drone alone destroyed an entire building, and trust me, that's not the most powerful thing I brought along."

"You're advocating for going after this guy?" Aaron crossed his arms. "You. The guy who snipes baseballs because he can't stand the sight of blood."

Jasper's face screwed up. "I thought I told you never to talk about that."

"You're afraid of blood?" Bertha cocked an eyebrow. "So that's why they shuffled you out of the marine corp."

"We're getting off topic." Aaron held up a hand as Jasper's fist curled. "We can't go after him. Frank, did that drone ever get to the other city, Lambspoint?"

Frank shook his head. "It died about half a mile out. Just cut out."

"See?" Aaron shrugged. "He shut down our drone, he knows we're coming. It would be suicide. Top strike teams have gone up against this guy and not come out alive."

"I, for one, second what our leader is saying." Bertha waved a hand. "I'm tired, and really don't want to try to sleep in a dusty hotel room with all you guys. Well, maybe you, Garmund. Not the rest of you, though."

"I just…" Jasper shrugged. "Part of me wants to try it. Why do you think I'm always the one who goes to the game rather than just watching it with you guys? I kind of like actually doing something."

"I'd rather hide behind my computer." Garmund held up a hand. "That's why I became a hacker in the first place. No people trying to kill you."

"That's three against, one for." Aaron crossed his arms. "Frank? Even if you vote for it, you'll-"

"I'm not just going to vote for it." Frank stood up out of his chair. His eyes burned in the low lighting, and

Aaron winced. He hated these I-knew-your-uncle talks. "I'm going to go do it. You know what? Your uncle would be *ashamed* of you. He gave you a second chance because you showed promise. He wanted to see if you would take a failing department and do something with it. Instead, all you've done is sit on your rear end and let it degrade even farther." He clenched his fists. "If I die trying to take this guy down, so be it. Once I lose this job, my kids are throwing me in a nursing home, and that may as well be death. I want to go out swinging. If you want to give up, by all means, go for it. Me? I'm taking the van."

Frank turned and marched out of the hotel room, letting the door bang shut on him. Aaron sighed deeply. The jab about his uncle had hurt, deeply. The rest of the team sat in uncomfortable silence as Jasper walked to the door.

"I already told you where my vote stands."

As he vanished into the new night, Garmund shook his head and stood up. "I'll be a monkey's uncle before I let that little sprite Jasper outdo me. Guess it's three to two now." He paused as he reached the doorway, turned, and frowned at Bertha. "And I really *don't* want to stay in a hotel with you. Just… Just saying."

He stepped out the door, and Bertha winked at Aaron. He raised his eyebrows in what he hoped was a disapproving look, and she stood up and clapped her hands. "I told you, I hate hotel rooms. If the van is leaving, I'd better be on it if I don't want to be stuck here."

Aaron took a single moment longer to stare at the inside of the hotel room. A huge part of him wanted to forget the whole deal and walk away. It was more than a huge part of him, every nerve in his body wanted to avoid walking out that door.

There was something, though, that remembered his uncle. He had already lost the respect of his parents, his siblings, his grandparents. If he lost his uncle, he would have no one at all. At that point, his life would be reduced to flipping burgers and playing video games. While the idea certainly didn't sound as bad as some, he knew that a large part of him would miss the team. He knew he would miss the iota of respect he had.

Slowly, feeling as if he had signed his own death sentence, he walked up to the door of the hotel and pushed the door open. Whatever happened that night, he had a feeling that he wouldn't forget it for a good, long time.

CHAPTER 8

Harold barreled through the streets of the town, trailing a long tail of zombies. Sharron's warning was beginning to make sense, now that he was on the road. He was faster than the zombies, but they seemed determined to follow him no matter what the cost. Given that he had at least twenty coming after him, it was going to be more than slightly difficult to ditch all of them at once.

He jogged down the main street, glancing at the stores as he passed them. Only a few still had intact windows, and most of them had movement within their dark interiors. The school was just at the end of the main street, past the abandoned pizza restaurant. He only had to make it a block farther, and he was there.

As he came up to the final intersection on the main street, he risked a glance towards the city park. Down the street, he could see the church, steeple rising high into the sky, with dozens of corpses wandering around it. A brief flicker of light glanced out of the stained glass windows, the glimmer of a candle. He knew it well, as the church kept multiple candles burning nearly all the time. That said, they were all up in the sanctuary, not in the stairwell. Maybe more survivors?

He almost turned to head that direction, but decided against it simply due to of the number of undead standing in between him and the building. A muttered groan sounded behind him, and he continued forward, angling towards the school.

He drew close to the school, glanced behind him, and swore as he noticed the sheer number of zombies following him. Without stopping, he risked a glance at the large, metal-plated front doors. He was quite certain that, in the light of the moon, he could see screws glinting where they had pushed through the door from the other side. If nothing else, it confirmed his suspicion that *someone* had taken up residence in the building.

After a moment of thought, he ran around the side of the building, gliding past the windows like he had done so many times when trying to slip in after the bell. There was a secret way to get inside without alerting any of the teachers, so long you did it right. Of course, "secret" was a bit of a misnomer. All the teachers knew about it, but as long as you weren't caught teaching the kindergarteners how to do it, they typically didn't care.

He soon reached the backside of the building, where he jumped upwards, grabbing ahold of a fire escape ladder. It slid down to ground level, and he scrambled upward. His feet touched the metal platform set about ten feet off the ground, and he pulled the ladder back up.

The three zombies still in his line of sight wandered up underneath the fire escape and stared up at him. Idly, he noticed that one of the three was a new zombie, a middle-aged woman he actually didn't recognize. Probably someone who had come into town from Garden City for the exhibit. Just like at the farm and on the porch, they didn't try to attack him any further, and simply looked at him.

Satisfied, he began to climb upward. They continued to follow him with their eyes until he reached the top level, at which point they turned and wandered away. Harold took a deep breath and crawled over the edge of the roof.

His feet hit the top of the roof, and a hammer clicked near his ear. He froze, frowned, and let out a breath.

"Really? I escape the zombies and you threaten to shoot me?"

"We don't know what your intentions are." The voice was deep and gravely. "You might be trying to steal our supplies or something."

"Mr. Harris?" Harold chuckled and turned around. "Come on. The dead started rising about four hours ago. That's not nearly enough time for society to completely fall apart."

"I'm glad someone else thinks so." Mr. Harris, the chemistry teacher, lowered his rifle. "Principle Gruen ordered all the watchers to thoroughly interrogate anyone who tried to come inside."

"Yeah, well, you can tell him to shove it." Harold shook his head. "That's acceptable at the end of the world, right?"

"You just started your senior year. We get things moving again, you're going to regret something like that." Mr. Harris shrugged. "That said, the guy is a huge prick. If you were going to tell him off, now would be the time."

"Perfect!" Harold started walking towards the door to the staircase. "Is he in his office?"

"No." Mr. Harris shook his head. "None of the rooms with outward-facing windows are being used. The headquarters are located in the locker rooms, at least for the moment."

"Man, someone's sure having fun with this whole thing." Harold chuckled. "I'm on my way."

He walked into the stairway, took a deep breath, and cranked open the rusty hinges. After wincing at how loud the noise was, he began to descend into the depths of the building. The school had three levels, which, in Harold's opinion, was two too many. The upper floor was used for the high school, the middle floor for the middle school, and the lower level for the elementary. Even with all three levels of education in the same building, there were still dozens of unused rooms filling the building.

Harold reached the bottom level, cracked the door open, and stepped out. No one threatened to kill him, and he walked down the hallway, feeling rather odd to be walking through the school during the night. It wasn't that he hadn't done it before, the abandoned rooms had made for some quite exciting late-night sabotage in years past. To actually be doing it with teacher knowledge was another matter, entirely.

A few moments later, he walked into the gymnasium. A handful of people sat around the bleachers, some of whom appeared to be sleeping in materials scavenged from the home living class. Two guards near the entrance to the locker room turned as he walked in, their hands going to shotguns sitting on nearby chairs.

"First off, I know you can't shoot that thing." Harold cocked an eye at the closest guard. "I've seen you shoot skeet before, and it's pathetic. Secondly, it's me. Harold. Lose whatever military dictatorship you're trying to pull and let me see Principle Gruen."

The first guard, a student named Jared, sighed. "You're the first person I've heard recently that actually sounds credible. Maybe you can talk some sense into him."

"Principle Gruen?" Harold chuckled. "The guy can be stiff, but he always seemed solid to me. Honestly, I'm kind of surprised he put all this together."

"Not him." Jared waved his hand. "That guy from the city, Kingsley."

"Great." Harold groaned inwardly. "I can just imagine. Thanks for the pass."

He walked past the guards and into the men's locker room. The familiar smell of sweat and showers rose in his nostrils, and he wrinkled his nose. If the zombies actually broke into the school, the doors to the locker room really weren't that great, not compared with the doors to the detention room. Not to mention the fact that since the undead couldn't climb, they'd be much safer at the top of the school. More problems to comment on.

As he walked into the larger part of the locker room, he was met with the sight of Principle Gruen sitting at his desk (which had apparently been important enough to risk a trip into a windowed room), talking with Kingsley, a student that nearly everyone in the building found insufferable.

Kingsley was… Interesting. He was a huge nerd, one of the most prevalent in the school. He could spend hours breaking down the latest episodes of various television shows, and, frankly, Harold rather enjoyed the in-depth analysis. The only problem was that he often started analyzing the real world in the exact same manner. And Harold *didn't* enjoy being told that the only reason he had lashed out at someone was because of an event that happened several weeks earlier.

Gruen and Kingsley both looked up as he walked in, and Kingsley's face screwed up. "I told you this is what would happen if we didn't increase security. Infidels walking into our haven, stealing our weapons."

"Relax, pipsqueak." Harold walked up to Kingsley and put a hand on his shoulder. On the desk in front of him were dozens of comics, books, and movies on the subject of zombies. Harold rolled his eyes and shook his head. "These are my own weapons, not yours. Studying up on our common enemy?"

Kingsley put his arms over the material. "Call it what you will, but people are fascinated with zombies for a reason. While some of these stories are undoubtedly more accurate than others, we can look at the common denominators and extrapolate from there."

"Or we can look at the real world, see the issues, and deal with the problem." Harold turned to Principle Gruen. "You're running this operation?"

"Yes, I most certainly am." Principle Gruen looked down at Harold, his bald head reflecting the dim lighting. "Kingsley is advising me. He came forth as the foremost expert in the town on the subject of zombies. I assume him to be our best chance of survival."

"What's he told you so far?" Harold crossed his arms. "They move slowly and try to eat you?"

"They devour any human flesh they can reach." Kingsley bit his lip and leaned forward. "They tend to move slowly, though there are accounts of them moving faster than a human could possibly run. Most of the time they possess inferior strength, and expand their population by biting people, spreading the virus."

"Not bad." Harold crossed his arms. "Here's what you missed. If someone dies, they reanimate. No need for biting or virus transfer. They move slow, but the longer they've been dead, the stronger they get. Strong enough to bust through walls, I should point out. Shoot them in the head and they die, miss and *you* die. Oh, and if you can climb on something, they lose interest and leave. I still can't figure out exactly how they track you. It sure seems like eyesight, but the really decayed ones don't have eyes."

Kingsley frowned. "That sounds like the accounts of Jim Paulo."

"Jim Paulo?" Harold frowned back. "Never heard of him."

"He was a Spanish missionary back in the fifteenth century." Kingsley began to sort through the comic books on the table. "He traveled to South America with Columbus, then split off from the main company shortly after they made land. He records fighting zombies, vampires, demons, and a whole lot more."

"And his zombies were similar?" Harold frowned.

"Very much so." Kingsley nodded. "Almost exactly what you described. He claimed to have found the cause of the zombies, along with the other demonic activity at the time, but the remains of his manuscript don't include exactly what it is that was found. At least, if they *did* exist, they were never published."

"Interesting." Harold mused. Maybe Kingsley wasn't so bad after all. "Did they mention anything about invisible barriers?"

"No." Kingsley frowned. "What do you mean?"

Harold explained the car crash and subsequent attempts to get around the force field surrounding the town. He crossed his arms, shifting his guns and making the principal jump slightly.

"Interesting." Kingsley mused. "Assuming that your memory is accurate, it almost seems to me that-"

Harold frowned. "My memory isn't accurate?"

Kingsley shrugged. "On the handful of occasions when you've been fortunate enough to secure a girlfriend, you've often wound up breaking up with her due to forgetfulness. Birthdays, anniversaries, the fact that her parents were scheduled to arrive on Friday, not-"

Harold scowled down the punk. *That* was why he couldn't stand the kid. Whose business was it why he had wound up breaking up with his past girlfriends? Besides, one-month anniversaries weren't *real* anniversaries.

"I'll have none of this." Principal Gruen mercifully cut in and prevented Harold from punching Kingsley. "This has passed the realm of bizarre and into the absurd. I want to know what in the world is going on and why."

Harold frowned. "Has anyone been by the church?"

Principle Gruen shook his head. "Not since the explosion. Why?"

"When I was running to the school, I saw a light down there." Harold shrugged. "Might be worth checking out."

"I'm not authorizing any trips out of this building." Principle Gruen shook his head. "We have around a hundred people in here. Figuring that fifty more were killed in the explosion, that only leaves couple hundred people scattered around town. Most of those are probably dead, which means that any scouts we send out are risking their necks for a population smaller than the number of people doing the searching. I'm afraid that I simply can't risk it."

"Then I'll go out without permission." Harold shrugged. "We have to figure out what caused this. Bernard was checking out a stranger that came into town right as this was happening. He was still here when the barricade went up. It's possible he might know something."

"I told you-"

Harold held up his hands. "Civilization and order are the first things to collapse when the apocalypse starts. I'm sure Kingsley can tell you the same thing."

Principle Gruen turned to Kingsley, who nodded. "It's true."

Principle Gruen shook his head and dropped into his chair. "Don't die, okay? The fewer deaths on my watch, the less my ratings drop when we come out of this."

Harold chuckled. "Death isn't in my plans."

"I'm sure it wasn't on the bucket list for anyone standing in that park, either."

Harold nodded at the sentiment, turned, and walked out of the locker room. He waved at the guards, swept out into the hallway, and made his way towards the staircase again. He had just reached the third floor when he heard a door bang in the lower levels. Footsteps pounded on the stairs, and Kingsley appeared next to him.

"What are you doing here?" Harold shook his head. "Shouldn't you be trying to figure out how to secure your position as a leader in the post-apocalyptic world?"

"Done. Be the sole supplier of food." Kingsley shrugged. "I've got a massive stash back home, along with a water purifier that people are going to need as soon as the city municipals break down."

"Great. You actually *have* thought this through."

"Look, I came to help." Kingsley crossed his arms. "I'm the fastest student on the track team, which means I can outrun those things. My dad taught me to shoot, so I'm at least decent with a weapon. Most importantly, I know Paulo's journals inside and out. I know what we're facing, how to kill it, and other random bits of information that I'm sure you would love to know."

Harold raised his eyebrow. "Like what?"

"Like the fact that the dead are reanimated by demons, not by a virus." Kingsley shrugged. "Granted, you already knew that it wasn't a virus, but you didn't know why they got stronger the longer they were dead. A newly-killed person still has too much life for the demon to be able to fully possess them. However, you only need a few hours before they get drained enough for the demon to work its magic."

Harold took a deep breath. "That means that the people who died earlier tonight will already have the full strength of the *really* dead ones."

"Exactly." Kingsley nodded. "If you hadn't known that, you would have tried to hide from a fresh one and gotten ripped to shreds. Now, are you ready to take me along, or not?"

Harold shrugged. "Fine. Tag along. Just don't expect me to pick up the pieces when you get ripped apart."

"Actually, I'm quite certain that you'll protect me. In the past, you've shown that-"

Harold did his best to tune out the prick as they ran towards the roof. They reached the top of the stairs and pushed the door open, stepping out into the night. Whatever they found, Harold hoped that they would be able to end it, and soon. The town, maybe even the world, depended on it.

CHAPTER 9

"Are we there yet?" Bertha whined from the back seat. "I'm tired and this van smells. And I'm sitting next to Jasper instead of Garmund."

"And here I thought we'd be safe from your complaining once we got out of the hotel room." Jasper muttered under his breath. "Can't you be positive about anything? Besides, *you're* the one who cleaned the van. If it smells-"

"Finish that statement, and you're going to regret it once we get back and I'm assigned to clean the men's room." Bertha's voice was cool. "And I'm positive that there's no way I'm staying in this vehicle longer than necessary. I mean, is there anyone here who particularly *wants* to be in here?"

"I'd take it over walking." Frank muttered. "I'd be willing to bet that no one in here is going to argue with *that*."

Aaron let out a long breath. He couldn't complain about space, since he was riding in shotgun, and by extension had more legroom than anyone else in the van. He just *really* didn't want to be on the trip. Frank glanced sideways at him, an odd look on his face. Aaron knew that the security guard was disappointed in him, but it was hard to know exactly why. Was he disappointed because Aaron hadn't wanted to come in the first place? Or was he upset because he knew that Aaron still didn't want to be there? It was impossible to figure out, Aaron just felt awful about it. He felt like he was letting the man down, something he had never particularly cared about before now.

He was still pondering it when something on the road ahead caught his eye. "Hey, Frank? You see that?"

"My technological skills are bad, not my eyesight." Frank slowed the van down to a crawl. "Looks like someone had quite the accident."

They drew to a stop about thirty feet in front of a wrecked sheriff's vehicle. It looked like it had collided against something large and immobile, but there wasn't a thing on the road.

"Dr. Incacheck's work?" Jasper mused. "I wonder what kind of weapon he used to do *that?*"

'Something tells me that we'll find out sooner rather than later." Aaron shrugged. "We're only half a mile outside of town. Well, the ditches don't seem too bad here. You can probably just pull around it."

Frank nodded, pulled into the shallow ditch, and sent the van through the tumbleweeds and sagebrush.

A strange electrical feeling rushed over Aaron's body, and he let out a yelp. With a blast, the van was propelled forward, blasting past the sheriff's car with a vengeance. The front end left the ground, only to come slamming back down in the ditch. Aaron was thrown forward, his seatbelt catching him securely. A moment passed as they skidded along the dirt, and the van came to a halt.

"What in the wide, wide world was that?" Bertha snapped. "Frank? I always told you that you shouldn't be driving."

"Wasn't me." Frank stomped on the gas pedal a few times and cranked the key. Nothing happened, as the engine simply emitted a series of clicks. "We went through some sort of field. Fried my engine solid. We aren't moving."

"Then let me out of this thing." Bertha held up her hands. "Out. Out!"

Aaron opened his door and climbed out, feeling the dust rise under his feet. If he hadn't known he was in Kansas, he would have sworn he was in the middle of a desert.

Behind him, the rear door slid open, and Garmund climbed out, stretching dramatically and yawning loudly. Bertha took advantage of the opportunity to bump into him, running her hands along his shoulders. Jasper crawled out after them, shaking his head at the display.

"Alright, time to weapon up." Jasper walked to the back of the van. "All of you! Get over here now!"

"You enjoy this part of the job way too much." Aaron shrugged as he walked to the back. "What do you have for us?"

"Well, not any of this computer stuff." Jasper pulled a large duffle bag out of the rear compartment. "Garmund, you might want to see if your toys still work."

Garmund grabbed the bag as a series of questionable words pouring out of his mouth. He unzipped the massive compartment while Jasper reached farther into the van.

"For our fearless leader, I bestow on you the duel pistols." Jasper pulled out two pistols on a belt and handed them to Aaron. "Just clip it around your waist, the auto-tightener will do the rest."

Aaron took the belt and did as he was told. Motors whirred as the belt tightened, and his gut protested wildly. It didn't want to stop tightening! As his stomach bulged out over it, Jasper's eyes went wide. He reached over to Aaron's side and slapped the side of the belt. The whir stopped, then started again as the belt loosened to a more comfortable diameter.

"Sorry about that. I had it calibrated for a fifteen-inch waist." Jasper muttered. "Alright, arms up."

"Why would you have it calibrated for a   waist?" Aaron frowned as he lifted his arms. "Were you trying to arm a supermodel or something?"

"Hey, you don't ask me about my life, and I won't ask you about your browser history." Jasper reached into the back of the van and pulled out a vest that was covered in holsters. "Which Garmund may or may not have hacked. Incidentally, do you do *anything* except play that old arcade game and watch anime?"

"I thought we weren't asking questions." Aaron frowned as Jasper slid the vest over his head. "What *is* all this, anyway?"

"I'm trying to get you outfitted." Jasper sighed and pressed a button, causing the vest to tighten down as well. Aaron counted over ten guns and dozens of extra rounds of ammunition. "I told you I was giving you dueling pistols. Never go into a duel without lots of extra back-ups."

"I'll keep that in mind." Aaron sighed as the vest continued to adjust itself, even changing what level the guns hung at. Once the vest was in place, Jasper turned to the rest of the team.

"Bertha! I'm trusting you with my second favorite weapon."

"What's that?" Bertha cocked an eye at him. "Does it make big explosions?"

"Nope. That's my favorite weapon that does that." Jasper pulled something that looked like a large rifle. Rather than a barrel, though, it had an odd-looking track that ran the length of the weapon. "This is a grenade launcher. Medium explosions. This thing can take out an entire room at a time, so be careful where you point it."

"I like it already." Bertha smiled and caressed the weapon. "Does it have a name?"

"That task can go to you." Jasper shrugged.

"Then I'm naming it Gar-"

"It works!" Garmund's voice echoed from behind them, and Aaron jumped. They turned to see the hacker standing up, doing a small dance. He drew up short and turned to face them, putting his hands behind his back. "All my stuff works. No adverse effects from whatever we hit."

"Good." Jasper muttered. "Now you can be carrying electronics instead of weapons."

"I'd still enjoy a weapon."

"I'd bet you would." Jasper shook his head. "Frank?"

Frank stepped around the vehicle. "Sorry. I was trying to see what was going on in town. You know, watching like I'm supposed to do?"

"See anything?" Aaron shrugged.

"Not a thing." Frank crossed his arms. "Which I find kind of an issue."

"What do you mean?" Aaron turned back to the weapons. "Not seeing bad things coming to kill us is usually a good thing."

"The problem is that I didn't see *anything*." Frank muttered. "The lights in the town are all off. It doesn't even look like there are vehicles driving around. You tell me what town doesn't have *some* sort of nightlife, and I'll take it back."

Aaron frowned. "It *is* only about ten o'clock. People should still be out and around."

"Exactly." Frank nodded. "All supporting my conclusion that something is up. The doctor is here, and there are problems." After a few seconds, he crossed his arms. "Not to mention the force field we just drove through."

"Well, get back to watching. Let us know if something's on its way." Aaron nodded at the guard. Frank's brow knit together, but he nodded back and walked back to the front of the vehicle.

"Wait!" Jasper held up his hand. "I didn't give you your weapon!"

When Frank failed to reappear, he shook his head, pulled out something that looked like a fire extinguisher, and stalked to the front of the vehicle. Aaron stayed at the rear for a few moments longer, shook his head, and started walking towards the front as well.

He got there just as Jasper was leaving. Frank looked down at the tank that was clipped to his belt, let the nozzle drop, and shook his head. "I don't understand all this newfangled weaponry. When I was in active duty, all that you needed to kill an enemy was a bullet."

"I think that's all you still need, technically." Aaron shrugged. "These get the same job done and are a whole heck of a lot more fun to play with."

"I guess." Frank shrugged. "I guess I just miss when things were simpler."

Aaron thought back to when he was in high school and could do everything he already did without the responsibility or expectations of being an adult. "Yeah. Me too, I guess."

He frowned as a scuffling noise rose in the air. "Do you hear that?"

"Hear what?" Frank frowned. "I don't... I can sure see something, though."

Aaron reached for his hip and pulled one of his pistols off his belt. Almost instantly, the smell hit him like a freight train. Decay, rot, the smell of his refrigerator after two months of forgetting to clean it out. A shape seemed to materialize out of the darkness, a shambling, stumbling individual that looked distinctly like a zombie.

As it drew closer, Aaron got a glimpse of flashing teeth, empty eye sockets, and grasping limbs. Without a second thought, he brought the gun up, aimed, and squeezed the trigger. The gun kicked in his hand, firing a powerful bullet. Of course, he missed by a mile, and proceeded to fire at the zombie three more times before he finally hit it between the eyes. The monster fell in a heap, and Aaron puffed out his cheeks for a moment.

The rest of the team ran up to him, weapons at the ready. Aaron gestured at the zombie with his gun.

"I killed it. No reason for panic."

Bertha bent down, wrinkled her nose, and took a few steps back as she stood up. "That thing came after you?"

Aaron nodded. "Not a huge issue, really. Just shoot for the head. Everyone who watches television knows that."

"You just got attacked by a *zombie!*" Bertha shook her head. "I'm out. This is too much. I change my vote."

With that, she turned around and started walking down the road, towards the town they had just come from. Garmund walked after her. "Wait!"

"Sorry, hon. I know you're all over me, but-"

A loud zap echoed through the air, and Bertha was thrown through the air, slamming into the rear of the van. Aaron held his breath as she twitched for several seconds before reanimating.

"A field that lets things in, violently, and doesn't allow them back out? What kind of hellhole is this?" Bertha snarled.

"We just got attacked by a zombie." Jasper held up his hands. "I'd say that we're in a pretty special kind of hellhole."

"Is no one besides me concerned by the fact that a corpse just tried to kill us?" Bertha crossed her arms. "Anyone?"

"The manual at the office actually covered what to do in the event of a zombie apocalypse." Jasper shrugged. "If you had ever read it, you'd know."

Bertha raised an eyebrow. "And did *you* read it?"

Jasper chuckled. "Not a chance! I started, but it was all charts and stuff. The new tv show was…" His voice trailed off in contemplation, and Bertha laughed.

"You people are pathetic."

"A: You're one of us. B: We're also being realistic." Aaron crossed his arms. "We're trapped out here. Shoot, we were going after Dr. Incacheck! If the worst he did was turn a town into zombies, I'm almost thankful. Other options on the list included an airborne pathogen that caused your lungs to burst, nuclear exposure to cause cells to mutate, parasitic-"

"I get the picture." Bertha held up her hands. "What do we do now?"

"If Incacheck is here, he's probably at the center of town." Aaron paused in thought. "These towns were nearly always built up around a church. Logic states that if we find the church, we find the doctor."

"Sounds good enough for me." Frank nodded. "That's the first sensible thing you've said today."

"Actually, I was going to suggest that we keep walking around the edge of town, see if there's a weakness in this shield. The note about the Doctor's location was so we could avoid it." Aaron shrugged. At Frank's disapproving glare, he threw up his hands. "Or we can run into a zombie-infested city and try to stop a crazed scientist."

"Good." Frank nodded and started walking down the road. "Let's move!"

"Wait!" Jasper ran back, only to reappear a moment later with the biggest gun Aaron had ever seen any single person carry. It was nearly two feet thick, three feet deep, with a barrel that extended well over six feet into the distance. "Okay, I'm ready."

"How in the world do you carry that thing?" Aaron raised an eyebrow.

"It's mostly empty space." Jasper shrugged. "Filled with gas."

"Flammable gas?" Bertha took a step away.

Jasper paused. "Electrifiable gas."

Aaron was quite certain that it was impossible to electrify gas, but he bit his tongue and simply walked into the darkness. If any more zombies decided to attack, it was going to be nigh-on impossible to see them ahead of time, which meant that he had to be listening with an intensity like none other. That was doable, he supposed. As an argument broke out between Bertha and Jasper, he took a few steps ahead. It was probably better to run into the zombies a bit quicker than to get caught up in the argument and not hear them at all.

CHAPTER 10

"There's the church." Kingsley whispered. "What do you see?"

"A bunch of rotting corpses. Nothing more." Harold whispered back. They were crouched in the bushes in front of the Carpenters' house, which directly bordered the park. Directly across the park, beyond a sea of trailers from the Smithsonian exhibit, was the massive church. The light that Harold had seen earlier was either gone, obscured, or had never existed in the first place.

"Can we get any closer?" Kingsley frowned. "We could use the trailers for cover."

"There are too many of them wandering around the exhibit." Harold grimaced as one of the trailers was knocked over, eliciting a number of loud crashes. "We'd never get through without being spotted."

"We could probably make a run for it." Kingsley shrugged. "They're pretty slow. I bet we could make it."

"Yeah, I've been thinking about that." Harold bit his lip. "It just makes me nervous. When they first showed up, a few of them were able to run after me. I haven't seen it since, but the possibility makes me nervous. Anything in your book about running zombies?"

"Not a word." Kingsley frowned. "Paulo notates that the concept of running corpses is almost comical. Walking corpses is interesting enough, but the idea that they could be capable of anything more than abstract motion-"

"Probably why we can just climb things to get away." Harold frowned. "I wonder if they could climb stairs?"

"I'd rather not be in a position to find out."

"Yeah, me either." Harold let out a long breath. "Alright, here's-"

A hand broke through the bushes next to him and grabbed onto his shoulder. He was pulled through the hedge, directly towards the mouth of a zombie that had slipped their notice. Its rotting jaw snapped open, and Harold slammed his fist into its chest.

Surprisingly, his hands went clear through the chest cavity and out its back. The zombie stumbled, and Harold dropped to the ground. The rotting fingers lost their hold on him, and he rolled away as fast as he could.

Kingsley jumped over the bush, grabbed his arm, and hauled him to his feet. "I think more are coming."

The zombie that had just grabbed him lurched forward, limbs grasping. Harold risked a glance towards the city park, where several more had noticed the commotion and started lurching in their direction.

They started to walk away at a slow trot, just faster than the shambling creatures. Harold let out a long breath as they jogged away from the park.

"I thought I was dead." He shook his head. "Thanks."

"All I did was pull you to your feet." Kingsley shrugged. "Nothing that… Oh, blast!"

Harold turned to see the zombie he had punched sprinting towards him. Without another word, Harold turned and put on as much speed as he could. Beside him, Kingsley matched him pace for pace. They ripped away from the park, heading east out of town.

More grunts came from the sides of them as they tore down the main street. Idly, Harold noticed that they were getting quite near to his house. He thought for a moment about checking on Sharron, but abandoned the thought as a dried finger scraped across his back. Before long, they were past his house, heading for the open road.

"We've got to figure something out, and soon." He gasped between footfalls. "Barrier coming!"

"Get down!" An unfamiliar voice echoed through the night. Harold had no particular intention of obeying the voice, but was forced to do so as his foot caught on a crack in the road. He fell headlong on the asphalt, feeling the pavement scratch at his cheek.

A blast of gunfire rang in his ears. A moment later, a hand grabbed his arm, pulling him upward. He fought it at first, before realizing that it wasn't a rotting hand doing the pulling. He looked up into the eyes of an aging man with a twinkle in his eye. He took a step back, glancing at his rescuers. Kingsley joined him as he scraped himself off the ground.

"You okay?" A slightly overweight man in a ratty t-shirt stepped forward and held out his hand. A moment later, he noticed that his hand was still holding a pistol, and hastily pushed the weapon back into the holster.

Harold gladly shook the hand. "Yeah, I think we're good now. My name's Harold, his name's Kingsley. Who are you guys and what in tarnation are you doing here tonight?"

Kingsley stepped forward. "You're equipped for war. You knew this was happening, didn't you?"

"Not exactly." The leader paused. "We're actually here for a different purpose. Have you ever heard of Dr. Incacheck?"

"The guy who took over the country?" Kingsley frowned.

"The other Incacheck." The leader shook his head. "Man, they had to make things confusing for everyone, didn't they?"

"Focus." The older man smiled. "We're from the Apocalypse Prevention Department, a division of the United States Military. My name's Frank, I'm the security guard who keeps track of everyone else."

"Apocalypse Prevention Department?" Harold chuckled. "You're a little behind the curve on this one. The apocalypse already started, and it's just getting worse."

"Then call us the Apocalypse Squad." The leader crossed his arms. "My name's Aaron. The guy with the big gun is Jasper, the guy with the duffle bag is Garmund, and the girl is Bertha."

"I'm the girl?" The lone female, presumably Bertha, shouted forward. "Of the two of us, which one ran screaming when that mouse got into the control room last week?

Aaron groaned and turned around. "I… Just… That's Bertha." He sighed. "Got it?"

"Nope, but I'm sure we'll recap later." Harold sighed. "Now, you were here after a doctor?"

"Dr. Incacheck." Aaron nodded. "He's a mad scientist known for experimenting on local populations. While we didn't know what he was doing, I think we can safely assume that he's in charge of this whole mess."

"Great." Harold crossed his arms. "Tell me what I need to do."

CHAPTER 11

Aaron looked down at the two teenagers. Oddly enough, though they had just came from town being chased by zombies, neither of them seemed particularly afraid. Harold looked like a worker, someone who had done a substantial amount of hard labor in his young life. The other, Aaron could have spotted a mile away standing on a street corner. He was a nerd, a fellow compatriot. Aaron knew that he would have to find some time to talk to the kid, but later, once things had settled down.

"What can you tell us about the zombies?" Aaron frowned as he looked up at the town. "Anything juicy?"

"They're insanely strong unless they *just* died." Harold frowned. "It also looks like some of them are gaining the ability to run. They couldn't do that when they first showed up."

"Showed up?" Aaron frowned. "Are we talking spawn points, a strange van rolled into town and let them out, or-"

"The graveyard just started coming to life." Kingsley shrugged. "I was at the exhibit when it happened."

"Exhibit?"

"Oh, yeah." Kingsley frowned. "There's a big Smithsonian exhibit in the city park. Anyway, we were just milling around when all of a sudden the zombies clawed their way up out of the grave. As I predicted would happen in such an event, despite being in low levels of danger, panic-"

Harold cut Kingsley off. "I was working on a farm when it happened. A bunch of unmarked graves from years past just came to life."

Aaron frowned. "Sounds like the zombies in Jim Paulo's journal."

"I said the same thing!" Kingsley grinned. "See? I'm not so strange."

"Someone else has read the same book." Harold shrugged. "I hardly think that makes you normal."

"I still knew something." Kingsley muttered.

Aaron let out a long breath. "If I'm not mistaken, Paulo's diary doesn't include zombies that can run."

"That's what Kingsley here said." Harold frowned and crossed his arms. "If they can move faster than us, we lose the one advantage we have over them."

"And if they evolve even farther, we lose a whole heck of a lot more than that." Aaron ran his hand through his hair. "What's the situation in town?"

Harold took a moment to sum up the situation at the school, the church, and his home. When he finished, Aaron nodded.

"That kind of confirms what we suspected. We make the church our target?"

"Sounds like a plan to me." Frank nodded. "We get this guy where it hurts."

"Hold on." Garmund let out a long breath. "Can we have a word? In private?"

Frank waved at them. "Go have your meeting. I'll stay with these guys."

Aaron nodded, and he and the other three other members drifted back a few paces. Garmund crossed his arms and shifted slightly.

"What are we doing?"

"The same thing we were doing a few minutes ago." Aaron crossed his arms. "We're going to get Incacheck."

"We're heading into zombies that are *evolving*." Garmund tried to wave his hands, but they were too bogged down with electronic equipment. After a few frustrated seconds, he just groaned and hmphed. "You tell me how that's a smart idea."

"Alright, I'll spell it out for you." Aaron let out a breath. "If there's a force field around this town, it's likely that Incacheck put it in place. Keeps people from escaping while he performs his tests."

"Your point?" Garmund cocked an eyebrow.

"If we hide and don't do anything, we're just going to stand by, waiting it out, while the zombies grow more and more powerful." Aaron crossed his arms. "By the time any other help comes, we'll have been crushed under some superzombie that we can't even hope to defeat. Our best chance at getting out alive is to charge into Incacheck's lair while his zombies are still relatively weak, blow him to kingdom come, deactivate the force field, get the national guard in here, evacuate the survivors, and drop a nuke on this town." Aaron raised an eyebrow. "None of which can be accomplished if we run and hide."

"Nuke?" Jasper snorted. "You guys have such small dreams."

Garmund just shook his head. "Why not just send a call out? Get help on the way now? That's what the military is for."

"We *are* the military." Aaron just shrugged, thinking of the way Harold had looked up at him. "And right now, we're all these kids have."

"Oh, so now you're some big hero?" Bertha chimed in, not coming in on the side that Aaron would have hoped. "Excuse us for treading on your toes, savior."

"I don't want to be a hero." Aaron shook his head. "I never have, but right now, we have no choice but to press onward. We may as well give these kids some hope."

Bertha crossed her arms and raised an eyebrow. "What happens when they find out what we really are?"

"What are we?" Aaron crossed his arms and turned to walk away. "We're the Apocalypse Squad. Nothing new about that."

"Actually, I *do* believe that's the first time we've ever gone by that name." Bertha held up a hand.

Aaron sighed and ran his hand through his hair. "Yeah, but it sounds good."

"Nope." Bertha's voice drifted forward as he started to walk away. "It really doesn't!"

Aaron ignored her, and soon reached the location where Frank was talking to Harold and Kingsley. Both teenagers looked up at him as he approached, and Harold crossed his arms.

"Done with your group huddle?"

"Yeah, I think so." Aaron nodded. "Shall we get moving?"

"Do I get a gun?" Harold glanced pointedly at Aaron's chest. "I had a shotgun with me. Get me back to the park and I can get it back, but I need something until then."

Aaron shrugged and pulled two of the pistols off his vest. It wasn't like he was going to use *all* of them. Harold happily accepted the weapons, and Bertha walked up behind him.

"You first, leader."

Aaron nodded. "Alright, move out! Shoot anything that moves that isn't alive. Dr. Incacheck, we're coming for you."

They took a few steps through the darkness before Frank spoke up.

"You do realize that talking to the villain from afar isn't going to do you a lick of good, right?"

Aaron shrugged. "It's always more epic in the movies."

"I'll bet." Frank muttered. "I can't stand those movies anyway. The old classics? Now those were something to watch. This new stuff? All the blood, gore-"

"Decent plotlines that have actual thought put into them." Aaron countered. "Come on. Those old westerns were just shoot 'em ups without any semblance of a plot. The villain's motivations weren't well-defined, and-"

"Does a villain always *have* to have a strong motivation?" Frank held up his hands. "Sometimes a crazed sadist is enough. Sometimes people are just jerks, or trying to prove their superiority. None of this early-life family drama that they add to everything nowadays."

"I'm with Aaron on this one." Kingsley spoke up. "Newer movies have more of an art to them. They craft the stories better, they-"

"Oh my goodness, can we put a lid on the critic section?" Bertha snapped. "We're surrounded by zombies, and all you care about are which movie is better."

"All you watch is that home and garden show on television." Aaron countered. "You have no room to-"

A scratching noise echoed on the road ahead of them. A series of clicks filled the air as guns rose. A zombie materialized out of the darkness, running at full-tilt. Aaron squeezed the trigger, feeling his gun kick in his hand. Dozens of shots rang out as everyone in the party fired. The monster dropped, and Aaron turned back to Bertha.

"Anyway, that show is trash as far as viewing goes. You can tell that they manufacture all the drama just for the sake of keeping you entertained. Shoot, it would be half the length if-"

"Guys?" Harold spoke up. "Zombies."

"We hit the last one." Aaron shrugged. "We'll hit anymore that show their ugly, rotting-"

"No." Harold pointed forward. "*Zombies*. A whole herd of them, are you even watching the road?"

Aaron turned his attention back to the matter at hand. In the distance, he could see a row of houses silhouetted against the sky, several football field lengths from their position. Between the houses, he could just barely see something moving, but it was nearly impossible to see anything in the gloom.

"I guess I can see something." Aaron frowned. "You're sure it's a herd of zombies?"

"I'm sure." Harold nodded. "They're holding position at the edge of town. Almost looks like they're trying to block us from coming back in."

"How can you see that?" Aaron squinted, trying to see the undead.

"I have to help Old Man Ferguson keep coyotes off his newborn calves at night sometimes." Harold shrugged. "You get used to seeing things in the dark."

"Incacheck knows we're here." Jasper stepped forward. "We've got him scared."

"Hold up." Aaron frowned. "If that's true, those zombies are being controlled somehow. Garmund?"

"I could scan for control frequencies if I had a decent place to set up." Garmund's voice was wary. "You know. Somewhere that's not actively being overrun. I'm not seeing that out here, though."

"You'd be fine to set up in the school." Harold stepped forward. "The only problem is that it's behind the line of zombies."

"Is there anywhere that *isn't* behind the wall of zombies?" Garmund sighed.

"The van?" Jasper gestured over his shoulder with this thumb.

"That said, there are a lot fewer zombies around the school." Harold shrugged. "Once we get through that first line, it should be smooth sailing."

Aaron frowned as he tried to think. "Okay, then. Harold, I want you to take Frank and Garmund back to the school. Garmund, get set up and start doing whatever you can to figure out what makes these zombies tick. Deploy the drones, too, I want as good a picture of this town as I can."

"What about-"

"The rest of us will attack the church." Aaron shrugged. "On the off-chance that we fail, it would be better to have some eggs in another basket. There's also the possibility that we get there and find out that Dr. Incacheck isn't there in the first place, in which case it might be better to have a head start on any control measures."

"Why do I have to go with them?" Frank frowned. "I can fight!"

"You also can't move as fast as the rest of us." Aaron held up his hands. "We need you somewhere you can help protect people."

Frank muttered something under his breath, but nodded.

"On it." Garmund groaned and stepped over next to Harold. "Lead the way."

"Actually, let us lead the way." Aaron let out a breath. "We'll break through the zombies, you can follow through the lesser-populated path we leave. Deal?"

"Ready, break." Garmund muttered sarcastically. "Let's just get this over with."

"Don't worry." Bertha sidled up next to him. "We'll be back together before long."

Aaron shook his head, took a deep breath, and turned to the rest of the team. "Jasper? Any chance your weapon there can clear us a way?"

"Oh, yeah." Jasper smiled. "Oh, I've been waiting for a nice field test. Here goes nothing."

Jasper stalked forward, heading for the zombie line. Aaron followed closely, not wanting to miss the action. As they drew closer, he could indeed see the line of undead, simply standing there and waiting for them to arrive. When they had gotten within a few hundred feet, the line surged forward, leaping and bounding across the distance to meet them.

With a roar, Jasper's gun cut loose. Multicolored streams of energy flowed from the barrel of the weapon, stretching across space like ribbons floating in a breeze. As the energy beams struck the zombies, rotting flesh was stripped from the bone like dust in the wind. Zombies collapsed, husks of what they had once been, providing a nice, safe passageway.

The gun shut down with a whir, and Jasper turned to them with a grin. "Told you it was a nice gun."

"We never doubted you." Aaron chuckled. "How long until it recharges?"

"Entirely too long." Jasper shrugged. "Now, if you don't mind my saying so, there are more coming. I suggest we run."

Aaron shrugged. "Alright, then. Charge!"

With that, the team tore into the town. As they passed the line, Aaron got a glimpse of zombies running at them from the sides, materializing out of gaps in homes and streaking towards the team.

Aaron only made it a block before his breath began to come in gasps. He was simply too overweight to handle a long sprint. Bertha seemed to be having similar problems, though Jasper and Kingsley had grins on their faces as they ran through the night.

"Guys!" Aaron gasped. "Can't… Run…"

Kingsley and Jasper slowed. Jasper pulled a pistol off his belt, dropped his massive weapon, and started shooting into the dark. "You two are pathetic. You expect to reach the center of town like this?"

Aaron stopped running, drew two pistols, and turned back towards where they came from. A rotting face filled his vision as a zombie jumped at him, its jaw snapping down towards his neck. Instinctively, Aaron pulled the trigger, blowing holes in the zombie's kneecaps.

Without any support, the creature fell to the ground, wrapped dried fingers around Aaron's leg, and started trying to bite his calf. Aaron kicked it in the head as hard as he could, relishing the feel of the skull caving in under his boot.

The moment he had it off him, he looked back up. Three sprinters were heading his way, arms outstretched. He brought his guns up, squeezing off shot after shot. It took him three bullets before he managed to hit the first one, sending it into a sprawling heap. The second one took two more bullets, and Jasper shot the third off him before he had a chance.

"These things are way harder to hit than they are in video games!" Aaron started walking down the street towards the church. "Bertha? You have a grenade launcher, right?"

"You know it." Bertha raised the beast to her shoulder. "Let them come."

They reached the central intersection before more zombies showed up. A group of five exploded out the front of a store window, scrambling to get at the squad. Only one of them appeared to have been dead for an extended length of time, the rest looked like they had only been killed and zombified that very night. Aaron winced at the sight of their still-moist flesh getting sliced wide open on the glass of the window.

Bertha fired a grenade in their direction, and Aaron felt the thump in his chest as a fireball consumed the creatures. A smile worked its way across his face, and he grinned. They were getting ahead of the undead. The rest of the walk to the church would be a piece of cake.

He could just see the steeple of the church rising a few blocks away as they came into view of the park. Kingsley stepped up next to him and gestured to the side. Aaron nodded, and the group slid to the side of a store, into the shadows.

"Alright, last time we were here, this place was completely overrun." His voice wavered ever so slightly, and Aaron winced. If the kid got cold feet now, they were toast. "I mean, you can see the church. Once we've gotten to the church, or if we get driven back, the school is on the other side of the park. Climb up the fire escape on the backside to get inside."

"What if any zombies see us?" Jasper held up his hands. "Do you have security there to help get rid of any unwanted guests?"

"The zombies can't climb." Kingsley shrugged. "Don't know why. Anyway, if anything happens to me, that's where you'll find your friends."

"Got it." Aaron nodded. "Nothing's going to happen to you, though. Ready to kick some undead butt?"

Kingsley nodded, and they stepped out of the shadows. Aaron walked towards the tall building, a sense of duty in his chest. They almost had Dr. Incacheck in their grasp! All they needed to do was make it into the church and not get killed.

A massive roar cut through the night, and a pounding sound echoed on the street in front of them. A zombie tore out of the darkness, feet slamming into the ground with the force of a hundred tanks. It stood well over ten feet tall and appeared to be covered in some sort of bone plating. To top it off, several odd tentacles seemed to be dangling from its hands, dragging on the ground. Aaron brought up his guns and cut loose, squeezing the trigger again and again.

The rest of the team did the same, and Aaron's jaw dropped as the bullets simply ricocheted off the monster. It leapt forward, slamming into the ground next to them, and swung its arms out. Aaron ducked under the blow, barely missing the massive, armored fists. The tentacles lashed across his back, not drawing blood, but stinging a good bit nonetheless. Up close, the monster was even more disgusting. Hollow eye sockets peered out from underneath a solid bone helmet, and smaller tentacles could be seen writhing between bone plates.

Before Aaron could do a thing, it slashed an arm past him, striking Kingsley in the chest. There was a muffled whoomph, and the boy went flying backward into the side of the store. The monster roared and bent down, mouth wide.

With nothing to lose, Aaron leapt in front of the zombie, put the barrel of his gun in its mouth, and squeezed. The gun barked multiple times, and the zombie collapsed. The bulk of the creature landed on Aaron's torso, knocking him to the ground, and he yelped.

"Shoot." Jasper's voice was tight. "We've got more incoming. Looks like at least two more armorboys, a dozen or so runners."

"Great." Aaron muttered. "We need to move, and now. Anyone willing to help me out?"

Jasper bent down, tugging at Aaron's arms as the screams of the zombies grew closer. A corpse materialized out of the night just as Aaron's legs finally popped free, and Jasper yelped as dead hands closed down on his shoulders.

Aaron pointed his gun through Jasper's legs and shot the zombie in the knee. It slumped down, dragging Jasper down with it. When it landed, its momentum threw it over the top of Jasper, giving Aaron a clear shot. He put a bullet in its head, then spun to face the onslaught.

"Bertha! Now!"

Bertha nodded and fired her grenade launcher. Aaron smiled at the sight of three runners vanishing in flames, though the brief glimpse he got of the two more armored beings didn't fill him full of confidence.

"Can anyone carry Kingsley?" Aaron bit his lip as he continued to fire. Both of his guns clicked empty, and he tossed them to the side as he drew two more.

"I've got him." Jasper threw the boy into a fireman's carry. "I vote that we retreat."

Aaron nodded, glanced around, and ran for a small doorway on the opposite side of the street. Massive feet pounded on the ground behind him, and he did his best to ignore his aching lungs.

He tore through the door with everything he had in him, throwing it open as quickly as he could. Bertha and Jasper exploded through a moment later, and Bertha slammed the door shut. Aaron slowed to a jog, noting that they were standing in what appeared to be the storage room for a small grocery store.

"Well, that was-"

A massive, armored hand crashed through the door, slicing past Bertha's cheek. She leapt away, a trickle of blood running down her chin, and tore past Aaron in a breeze. Aaron followed as fast as he could, hearing the crashing noise of the zombie echoing through the abandoned corridor.

They ripped through the storage room at a speed that Aaron knew he would never be able to duplicate again, reached a door on the other side, and threw it open as quickly as they could. Hands reached through the door and latched down on Aaron's shoulders, and he fired his guns into the darkness ahead of him without thinking. The zombies collapsed, and he charged forward.

Jasper slammed the door shut just as Aaron heard the armored zombie finally break into the storage room. He glanced around, noting that they were now standing in a narrow alley between two stores. Without pausing to stop, he ran forward, threw open the door to the next building, and ducked inside. Bertha and Jasper followed him, shutting the door just before he heard the armored beast hit the inside of the grocery store door.

"Alright, we've got multiple barriers between us." Aaron let out a breath and began to walk forward, pushing aside several racks of cloth. "He shouldn't be able to find us."

Bertha blew past him without a second thought. "Yeah, but that one can."

Aaron turned to see another armored zombie crashing through the front window of the store. Jasper followed Bertha, and he did his best to stay tight on their tail. The zombie tore through the front store counter like it was nothing, smashed through the storage shelves, and honed in on Aaron.

In front of him, Bertha threw open the door out of the building and vanished into the night. Jasper vanished a moment later, leaving Aaron fighting to stay ahead of the monster's grasp. He was only feet from the door when a massive hand batted him to the side, tossing him into the doorframe.

Another hand came down on his leg, and several tentacles wrapped around his thigh. He collapsed and grabbed at the concrete, trying to gain some sort of hold, but it was to no avail. He glanced back to see the creature's jaw, open wide, ready to bite down on his leg.

With a roar, the first armored zombie exploded into the room. It slammed into the second zombie, simultaneously sending it sprawling and slicing off its hand in the process. The severed appendage let go of his leg, though the tentacles were still wrapped around him tight enough that it failed to simply fall free. He scrambled away as fast as possible, dragging the flopping hand.

Outside the building, he found himself facing a large, grassy expanse. Several large pieces of equipment pushed up out of the ground. Aaron drew up short, belatedly realizing that it was simply play equipment for a schoolground.

The presence of the school clicked in his head, and he charged forward, towards a large building that loomed out of the gloom. Behind him, he heard the building shatter as one of the behemoths broke through. A merry-go-round went flying past his head, and he swerved to the left, away

from the playground. No sense giving the zombie more ammunition to use against him. As he ran, he glanced desperately at the school. Kingsley had said to use a fire escape. He only had to find it.

After a few moments, he located the escape. Jasper and Bertha were already nearly three-quarters of the way up, doing their best to haul Kingsley with them. On the roof, someone started shooting, shot after shot, none of which did a lick of damage against the monster chasing Aaron. At least, he never heard the thud of a body, which made him assume that there was no damage done. Thankfully, as he drew closer to the exit, the tentacles around his leg finally loosened enough to fall free, giving him far more mobility. With a burst of speed, he pushed forward.

Jasper, already on the stairs, tossed Kingsley to Bertha and began running back down towards the bottom level. When he reached the lowest metal platform, he laid down on his stomach and let his hands hang down.

Aaron reached the rungs of the ladder and threw himself upward. Jasper's hands latched onto his wrists and hauled him upward, pulling him onto the platform. Aaron risked a glance backward, just in time to see a massive hand come crashing into the platform. The metal bent and Jasper fell backward, away from the school.

Aaron threw his arm outward, and Jasper grabbed ahold. For a few moments, Jasper hung there, massive zombie snapping below him. Aaron screamed as he pulled as hard as he could, dragging the man back upward. Jasper used his free hand to reach skyward, grabbing ahold of a now-dangling support. A moment later, he was able to pull himself back onto the twisted platform and crawl onto the stairs that led upward.

Aaron followed him, glancing down at the zombie. For whatever reason, the creature seemed to have given up, despite the fact that it could easily have reached up and ripped the escape from the side of the building. Aaron frowned in thought, not disappointed in the slightest by the revelation.

When he reached the rooftop, he collapsed onto the asphalt, feeling his lungs heave. Jasper knelt down next to him, and Aaron leaned forward.

"Where's Kingsley?"

"The guard took him." Jasper shrugged. "We're on duty until he gets back."

"Great." Aaron sighed and did his best to sit up. Jasper helped him, and Aaron took a deep breath. "You lost your big gun, didn't you?"

"It's sitting back in the street where I left it." Jasper nodded. "Man, I loved that gun. We'll have to see what they have around here to compensate."

"If you can manage to make a weapon with stuff you find laying around a school building, I'll be truly impressed."

"Prepare to be amazed, then." Jasper shook his head. "I'm just happy those things give up when you get above them. If they didn't, they could tear their way straight into this building."

"Given their recent adaptations, I'm not ruling out a climbing evolution." Aaron shook his head. "Ahh, this is awful. We can't get close to the church because of those things. Any ideas?"

"A few." Jasper nodded. "That tank Frank is carrying is an acid blaster. That could help get rid of a few, but it's going to run out after only a handful of shots."

"Any chance you could make some more acid?" Aaron shrugged. "I'm sure this school has a chemistry lab."

"Not one that you could do much with." Harold stepped out of the stairwell and stepped up to the group. "We once had a pretty good stash of nitroglycerin, but that all got used up during a… Well, it got used up on the first day of school. You'll find the crater out in the field beyond my house."

Jasper just grinned and rubbed his head, readjusting his beanie. Which, *somehow*, was still on his head. "Can you take me to the chemical depository? I can see if I can salvage something."

Harold nodded. "Sure thing. Aaron, Garmund is set up in the gymnasium, you'll probably want to see what he found. How close did you get to the church?"

"Not very." Aaron sighed and forced himself to his feet. "Those things are evolving faster than we thought. We need to come up with a new way to kill them, and quickly."

"Like I said, you'll want to talk to Garmund." Harold shrugged. "Weapons guy? This way."

As they walked through the door, Aaron took one more look out at the town. They were trapped behind the worst enemy lines he could conceive of. It was looking more and more hopeless every moment that they were there.

The worst part was that, once they were dead, Dr. Incacheck would have an army that he could use to crush the world as they knew it. Regardless of what he thought of their job, they *were* on the front lines of a potentially worldwide apocalypse. If it ever went beyond the barrier, there was little the world could do to stop it.

CHAPTER 12

"So, what do you guys usually do?" Harold glanced at Jasper. "I mean, do these kinds of things happen often?"

Jasper pursed his lips. "More often that you'd like to think."

That statement had to be true enough. Harold didn't *ever* want to think about a world-ending event, and yet, here he was. That was one time too many for him.

"What else have you guys dealt with?" He frowned as they walked onto the third floor of the building. "Vampires? Werewolves? Or are zombies pretty much the extent of it? I mean, I never would have thought zombies would be a thing, so I don't know which ones are real and-"

"I'm afraid that's classified." Jasper shrugged. "I could tell you, but then I'd have to kill you."

"That's the cheesiest line in the world." Harold let out a breath but kept walking.

He couldn't tell what it was, but there was *something* off about the Squad. They obviously had access to military equipment, and they were sure giving it everything they had to try and contain the apocalypse, but for some reason, he was almost positive that they were hiding something.

There was also the fact that the zombies themselves didn't seem to make any sense. Kingsley had been convinced that they were actually demons, and Aaron had seemed to confirm the fact, but yet the squad persisted in assuming that the creatures had been created by Dr. Incacheck. As far as Harold knew, the doctor may have been trying to use or control the demons, but there were just too many variables to decide what was and wasn't happening.

After a few more moments of thought, Harold shook his head and just kept walking. Whatever was happening, whatever the squad was or wasn't up to, they were the only ones with the firepower and experience needed to kill the zombies. That, at least, made them valuable.

"Alright, we're here." Harold grasped the doorknob, and, unsurprisingly, found it locked. "Give me a second."

"I can just smash through the door." Jasper rubbed his hands together. "Just…"

Harold walked over to a nearby air vent, stuck a finger through the narrow gap, and fished a key out of the dusty vent. "No need."

As they walked into the small lab, Jasper began moving from cabinet to cabinet, frowning at the labels.

"Not much selection here, but I think I can piece something together."

"You're pretty good with this stuff." Harold frowned. "Chemistry, weapons. Where'd you get all that?"

"My dad." Jasper opened a cabinet, frowned, and started pulling out bottles. "Well, kind of. He was a swordsmith, one of the best in the world. He would make blades for hobby fighters, the occasional sword nut, a few jilted lovers. There wasn't a huge demand for them, but the people who wanted them were willing to pay a *lot* for a quality blade."

He stopped talking as he grabbed several beakers and started tossing powders into the container. "Anyway, he sold a bunch of the swords to a group that put themselves forward as a group of high-risk entertainers. After they had been gone a couple months, we got a knock on the door from the government saying that a group of insurgents in the middle east had used the swords to attack a bunker of soldiers. Interestingly enough, the government wasn't interested in locking him away, they were interested in buying more weapons from him. Apparently, they were surprised that his swords could cut through bulletproof armor."

Harold chuckled. "How'd he manage that?"

"If I don't tell anyone my secrets, no one else can duplicate them." Jasper glanced over at him and grinned. "My dad had a few extra ingredients he would mix into the steel as he forged the blades. Once he went to work for the government, he had access to pretty much any and every chemical compound ever made. He started making bullets out of the same metal, working on armor-piercing rounds that could take down a tank. Before long, he had adapted the technique to pretty much all weapons. Ahh, those were the days."

Harold frowned. "What happened then?"

"That, my friend, is the reason I'm here now." Jasper crossed his arms and looked up from his creation. "In the end, he was supplying the government with unbeatable weapons. The issue was that he refused to give them the secret to his success, making himself invaluable. That little bit of information leaked, and a small Turkish hit squad made sure that the government could never use his help again. The government came to me next, and here I am."

Harold held up his hands. "You're not designing weapons for the government."

"No." Jasper grimaced. "No, I'm sure not."

Harold opened his mouth to pry farther, but the door was flung open to reveal Mr. Harris standing there, a look of incredulity on his face.

"What is this?" He stepped into the room, spinning around. "This is my stash of-"

"Right now, I don't rightly care." Jasper started mixing several powders together, then added a drop of liquid. Smoke belched upward, and he swirled the flask as the compound transformed into a brownish liquid. "We're facing the end of the world, and if I can't come up with a way to kill something that's already dead, we're going to feel its wrath."

"You could have just said so." Mr. Harris muttered. "What exactly are you creating?"

"I'm trying to build a bomb." Jasper shrugged. "This here is a secondary compound that I'll mix with a stabilizing agent, then add some-"

"What are you even talking about?" Mr. Harris walked up to the beaker and frowned. "None of these chemicals should be reacting with one another."

"And yet, they are." Jasper crossed his arms. "Look, I've been dabbling in explosives and weapons creation my entire life. I know a few tricks that the average person probably isn't going to have access to. Just trust me, okay?"

"Trust you." Mr. Harris muttered. "Give me one good reason why I should."

A roar sounded from outside the building, and Harold winced. Jasper pointed in the direction that the roar came from.

"Because right now, the only reason this building hasn't been overrun is because they don't know that we're inside. If we don't find some way to take them out, it's only going to be a matter of time before one of them grows tall enough that it doesn't care about the escape route. Or it could be a flicker of light through one of the windows that draws a curious one. Either way, we're only safe here for a brief amount of time."

Mr. Harris sighed. "Fine. You mind telling me what you're making?"

"Not at all." Jasper grinned. "At the moment, I'm working on a compound known commonly as PETN. It has a more complex scientific name, but-"

"PETN." Mr. Harris's eyes opened wide. "Pentaerythritol tetranitrate. That's one of the most explosive substances known to man."

"I happen to know a few that are stronger, but lack the materials here to create them." Jasper shrugged. "But yes, it'll cause quite a mess once I'm done. Then again, isn't that the point?"

Mr. Harris swallowed visibly. "How much are you going to make?"

"Enough to level a small town, if necessary."

Mr. Harris nodded slowly, turned, and walked out of the room without another word. Harold followed the teacher with his eyes, then glanced back at Jasper.

"How hard is it to learn to do all this stuff?"

"You ever bake a cake?" Jasper shrugged. "Similar concept. You just have to know what to add, and when."

Harold started pacing up and down the length of the room. "You need any help?"

Jasper paused for a moment. "I've pretty much got the PETN production down, but I suppose I could use some help with cooking up some flamethrower fuel."

Harold grinned. "Great! What do I need to do?"

CHAPTER 13

"Talk to me." Aaron walked up to the array of computer monitors that now filled a corner of the gymnasium. "What's the situation?"

"I launched the drones." Garmund frowned. "We've got a pretty complete picture of the town, and it's not overly pretty."

"Notice that I'm *not* the one doing the watching." Frank muttered. "I'm the security guy, but-"

"Can it." Aaron muttered. "We probably only have a few more hours before those things turn into another iteration that's even harder to beat. Garmund, go."

Garmund sighed and nodded. "Well, for starters, the field does indeed surround the entire town. It forms a perfect dome over the top of us, and even extends down into the ground. Nothing is going to break through without a significant amount of power."

"How much power are we talking?" Aaron frowned. "Something we can get out of a few batteries, or something we'll need a nuclear bomb for?"

"If we had a nuclear bomb, we *might* be able to break through." Garmund shrugged. "Of course, that would kill anyone inside the barrier, but… Details. Don't tell Jasper or he might try to figure out a way to do it anyway. This field is insanely strong. The bigger issue is that I'm not sure we would want to break out right now."

The computer screen lit up with pictures of zombies milling around the church. Nearly all of them now sported the bone plating, though several of them only had parts of themselves covered. Aaron grimaced as he realized that he could see the bone growing, filling the gaps with a speed that seemed unnatural. To top it off, most of the larger zombies seemed to be growing more of the tentacles as well, snake-like appendages that dropped from their hands.

"These things are getting more and more powerful. If we break out, they'll be unleashed on the world." Aaron breathed. "Any good news?"

"Two bits." Garmund hit a few keys, and the screens changed to show an overhead view of the town. "The first bit is that I've pinpointed the exact center of the barrier around the town, which, based on the patterns of the magnetic fields, seems to be the source of the field itself."

"The church." Aaron nodded. "Isn't it?"

"Nailed it." Garmund nodded. "The basement of the church, specifically. The other piece of good news is that I've located another group of survivors."

"Where are they?" Aaron frowned. "Anywhere good?"

"Better off than we are." Garmund chuckled and pointed towards the north side of town. "They're holed up in a bar over here. Looks like there's about fifty of them, and they've been taking down a *lot* of the zombies. Granted, they've only seen the stumblers and one or two of the runners, but-"

"Wait." Aaron pointed at the screens. "The zombies out there aren't evolving?"

Garmund frowned. The screen changed as he ran some computations, and he shook his head. "The only times the zombies evolve is if they're inside the city park or churchyard. Must be something that Dr. Incacheck has set up. Don't know if that helps us or not."

"It gives us a clue, at least." Aaron let out a long breath. "Can you get any drones close enough to the church to see inside?"

"Tried it multiple times." Garmund nodded. "All the windows either open into abandoned rooms or have some sort of black paint all over them. We aren't going to be able to see inside anytime soon."

"He's probably worried about his own creations turning on him." Aaron ran his hand through his hair. "Do we know yet how these zombies track people? Sight? Sound? Some other sense we're ruling out?"

"I think it must be some other sense we're ruling out." Garmund shrugged. "Most of these old corpses don't have any eyes or ears left to use. However these things are navigating, it's not any conventional method."

"Great." Aaron groaned and shook his head. "Well, I'd say that we have two primary goals. Kill all the zombies, and make sure the other group of survivors is safe."

"Like I said, I think they're a lot better off than we are." Garmund shrugged. "If we find a way to take out the monsters around here, we'll keep this other group from seeing any significant action."

"Sounds like a plan, except..." Aaron frowned. "You know, we could sit up on top of the school and shoot the things, and they would never be able to get up to us."

"That's true." Garmund nodded. "The only issue with that is that they'll also know where we are if they evolve much farther. If they get taller than the school and don't *have* to look up to see us, they could kill us all in an instant."

"That's true." Aaron shook his head. "Do we have a head count on the total number of zombies in the city?"

"That, we actually do." Garmund nodded. "There are one hundred fifty-seven more zombies left in the town. Fifty-three survivors at the bar, and seventy-eight survivors in the school. Not great odds, but we outnumber them for the most part."

"I want constant updates on those numbers." Aaron forced himself to his feet. "I'm going to go see how Kingsley is doing. Keep monitoring things, I want to know the moment that anything changes."

Aaron nodded to Frank, who nodded tightly back. Aaron stalked across the gymnasium towards the women's locker room, where he had been told the infirmary had been set up. The guards at the entrance nodded at him, and he stepped inside.

It felt odd, even in the apocalyptic scenario that they were facing, to walk into a women's locker room. As much trouble as he had gotten himself into in high school, that had been one area that had been strictly off-limits. It took him a few moments to shrug off the feeling as he walked into the main area of the locker room.

A tall, bald man stood in the center of the room, pacing back and forth. He spun to face Aaron the moment that he entered, a frown creasing his face.

"And you are?"

"Aaron." Aaron held out his hand. "My hacker and guard are set up in the gym, you-"

"Ahh, yes. Apocalypse Squad." The man shook his head. "A grandiose name if I ever heard one. Principle Gruen, by the way." Aaron held out his hand a second time, which the principal continued to ignore. "I understand that your group specializes in preventing world-ending events."

"We typically have better luck than this." Aaron shrugged. "We're working on a way to stop this, though."

"Oh, you are?" Principle Gruen stalked towards him. "And you're using my school to do it, I suppose."

"Unless you have any better place for us to go, yes." Aaron crossed his arms. "You have the most heavily fortified location in town, it would be stupid for us to operate out of anywhere else."

"I do have an eye for the best things." Principle Gruen smiled smugly, then frowned again. "Now, how exactly do you plan on stopping this?"

"Simple, really." Aaron shrugged. "Kill all the zombies, and then there's nothing to stop us from marching right up to the church and arresting Dr. Incacheck."

"Dr. Incacheck?" Principle Gruen took a step back. "The guy who blew up a town because a waitress gave him the wrong appetizer for his dinner?"

"No. Other Incacheck." Aaron waved his hand. "The younger one."

"Oh." Principle Gruen sighed in relief. "That's good."

Aaron held up a hand. "Excuse me. Zombies? He's obviously not a great person!"

"I suppose." Principle Gruen waved his hand. "So, your plan is to kill all the zombies. What happens when you miss one?"

"We'll deal with that when the time comes."

Principle Gruen paused. "I'm really not sure you're getting the picture here. You see, you're on my territory right now. There's nothing to stop me from simply throwing you out into the world, which means that I need incentive to let you stay. Your little plan doesn't exactly sound foolproof, which means that I need a little extra incentive, now don't I?"

Aaron paused, scratched his head as he thought about how to respond, then walked up to the principle. "You want incentive? Here it is. I don't know if we can help you survive this. Honestly, this is the worst situation we've ever seen in our years here. What I can tell you is that you won't survive without our help. No amount of money, no amount of weaponry, is going to help you when you're dead. Your only hope is to trust us, so you had better buckle down and get with the program, otherwise, we're going to evacuate you from your own building."

"Oh, I'm so afraid." Principle Gruen waved his hands in the air. "The mighty protectors of the Earth, throwing one of their charges out to the wolves."

"It wouldn't be the first time." Aaron growled. It was a lie, of course, but wasn't that what a movie hero would say in the same situation?

Principle Gruen's eyes widened, and he walked out of the locker room. Aaron shook his head, turned, and walked into the shower area. Inside, cots had been set up, filling nearly the entire space. Only one of the beds was in use, a cot near the door that held Kingsley. His eyes were shut, and blood oozed from a nasty-looking cut on his chest.

"I heard what you said to that guy." Bertha walked up and sat down on a nearby cot. "Not too shabby, if you ask me. One might even think that you were enjoying this job."

"I've seen too much television." Aaron shrugged. "Act tough, and it all falls into place."

"I guess." Bertha shrugged. "I don't know. Honestly, I'm about done with this nightmare."

"You and me both." Aaron sighed, glanced around the corner, and turned back to Bertha. "It's just… These people think we're actually *something*. This is the first time in my life that anyone has looked at me as more than just a screw-up."

"You don't want them to find out the truth?" Bertha cocked an eyebrow. "That their future is in the hands of dweebs?"

"I know what I would want in this situation." Aaron shrugged. "I would want someone to stand up for me. Maybe we can be that someone."

"How?" Bertha chuckled. "You ran like a girl when that armored zombie came after you. All that talk about reaching the church, and one zombie later, we're on the run. Talk is cheap, hon."

"You know what?" Aaron threw up his hands. "I don't know. I have a sick feeling in the pit of my gut that makes me want to vomit. I'm so afraid, I'm tired, and I have no interest in being here at all. You think we can let them see that?"

"Yeah." Bertha held up her hands. "Duh. If I was in this scenario, I would want to know that my protectors could use help. That way, I would know to run the first chance I got."

"Where would anyone run to?" Aaron matched her gaze. "There's nowhere to go."

"That's true, I guess." Bertha sighed, then cocked an eye towards the locker room entrance. Her voice raised, ever so slightly, and she flashed Aaron a coy grin. "At least I'm trapped in here with Garmund. It makes this terrible situation so much better."

"Well, no matter how good it is, the situation is about to get worse." Garmund appeared in the entrance of the showers, glancing uncomfortably in Bertha's direction. "I'm detecting energy surges from within the church. I don't think we have much longer before the good doctor does something extreme."

Aaron groaned and climbed to his feet. "Alright. Rally the troops. We move out in five."

"Just what are we going to be doing?" Garmund cocked an eyebrow. "You plan on sitting down for tea with the zombies and convincing them not to eat us like a scone?"

"Nope." Aaron shook his head. "We have to make it to the church, and quickly. I want you on surveillance, everyone else on the roof."

"Excuse me?" Garmund crossed his arms. "I thought you wanted Frank on surveillance."

"Normally, I would." Aaron glanced at the floor. His mind whirred, but he knew that he had to make a call. "Frank can't operate all your hacking stuff, though."

Garmund frowned. "You want me hacking?"

"I want you to hack whatever government servers you have to." Aaron nodded. "Call for help. Get real forces down here, stat. It's the only way we have a chance."

Slowly, he glanced over at Bertha. He expected to see some sort of acknowledgment on her face. Instead, all he saw was disappointment. Hadn't she just been advocating for leaving? Or at least telling the truth?

"And the rest of you are just going to charge the church?" Garmund raised an eyebrow. "Just like that?"

Aaron took a deep breath, a sense of sickness and death coming over him. "Yeah. This time, we're not stopping until Incacheck sees our faces."

CHAPTER 14

"And there we have it." Jasper put a cork in the flask and swirled the now-clear liquid a few times. "One bottle of liquid flame, ready for action."

Harold grinned widely. He had taken chemistry before, but it had always seemed so dull. Jasper made the concept exciting, a whirlwind of chemicals and mixtures that did who-knew-what. At the end of it, they had almost fifteen bricks of explosives and dozens of flasks and two-liter soda bottles filled to the brim with flamethrower fuel.

"I just hope this works." Harold rubbed his hands together. "What do I get to carry?"

"Right now, you get to take the bricks of explosives and run them down to the basement of the school, if it has one." Jasper shrugged. "Just in case we need to abandon the place."

"What?" Harold frowned. "You would blow up the school?"

"Not with people in it." Jasper frowned in thought. "We're probably going to need to take out a lot of zombies at once, eventually. The best way to do that, at least as far as I can figure, is to lure them all into a building and detonate enough explosive force to send the monsters into orbit. I figure we plant the explosives, and hope beyond hope that we never have to use them."

Harold nodded. "Got it. Do you want them all in one stack, or spread out?"

"All in one stack." Jasper nodded. "You can do more total damage if you spread them out, but I really don't want a large area of moderate damage. I want one specific area to be totally annihilated."

"I'll do my best to make sure that's what you get." Harold grinned. "Thanks. I really appreciate your letting me help you."

"Hey, that's what we're here for." Jasper shrugged. "We may as well give you guys the tricks you need to survive in the future, you know?"

"Yeah, I guess." Harold picked up several of the bricks. "I'll be back for the rest."

"Take several trips if you need." Jasper waved his hand. "We're in no particular rush at the moment. I'll just start moving these-"

"Jasper!" Bertha's head poked through the door. "We need to move, and now!"

"What's up?" Jasper looked up, not gathering his fuel any faster than before.

"Aaron called a meeting on the roof. We're attacking the church."

"Didn't we already do that once?" Jasper crossed his arms. "Oh, yeah, we did. He turned and ran like a little girl, as I remember."

"We all did." Bertha stepped up and whacked him on the back of the head. "Now move! We're going to need whatever you cooked up."

Harold held up his hand. "What about-"

"He would love your help too, if you're willing to give it." Bertha nodded. "Meet us on the roof. You have five minutes."

Bertha swept out of the room, and Jasper turned to Harold.

"You have five minutes to move all that stuff to the basement. Here, take this." He handed Harold a small pin. "Stick this in one of the bricks when you get down there. It's a remote detonating pin, I control the switch from my cell phone. That way, we can blow it anytime we want as soon as things go bad."

Harold took the pin, slid it in his pocket, and nodded. He then picked up several more bricks and ran as quickly as he dared for the stairwell. From there, it was a simple matter to make his way into the basement of the school.

Once he was there, he took a deep breath. Numerous superstitions surrounded the school basement, including rumors of murders, ghosts, and magic homework gnomes. All Harold knew for sure was that it was the sight of much promiscuity during school hours, which meant that he often steered clear of it.

At one point in the school's history, the basement had housed the locker rooms for the gym, presumably in order to make the changing rooms more private. However, after several wet-from-showering students had slipped and gotten concussions on the stairs, they built the new locker rooms above, next to the gym on the ground level. The old rooms remained, though, a labyrinth of possibility for anyone who dared to make the descent.

Harold frowned, trying to get his bearings. After a moment, he ran through several narrow, twisting corridors and drew up short next to a small storage closet. If he was right, the closet was directly underneath the middle of the gymnasium. Assuming Jasper wound up using his plan, and zombies did wind up overrunning the school, presumably most of them would wind up in the gym.

He set the pile of bricks in the middle of the floor, turned, and tore back towards the staircase. He flew up the stairs, three at a time, and exploded onto the third level with a vengeance. It took him a matter of moments to scoop up the rest of the bricks and make his way back down to the basement, completing his pile of explosives. With a flair, he pressed the pin into the explosive block, took a deep breath, and closed the door.

A set of dried, rotting hands lurched out of the darkness and latched onto his shoulders, dragging him forward. He caught a single glimpse of hollow eyes before a decayed jaw bit down on his shoulder. In an instant, it felt like molten lead had been poured into his body, filling his veins. He could only see one single eye, bearing down on him like a crater. Desperate, he tried to fight back, but found his limbs unable to move. Thunder pounded in his head as his body hit the floor, but he was unable to do anything more than scream.

Like a waterfall, the pressure and pain vanished in an instant. He gasped, inhaling deeply, and sat up. The zombie lay on the ground next to him, head disintegrated. Slowly, Harold turned to see Jasper standing in the hall, a concerned look on his face.

"You okay?" Jasper knelt down next to him. "Man, that thing has a nasty bite."

"It sure didn't tickle." Harold muttered. "I can't really see it. How bad is it?"

"Not awful." Jasper frowned. "It broke skin, but barely. It looks like this one was so far rotted that its bottom jaw broke from the effort of trying to bite."

"That's something." Harold took a deep breath. "Blast. Don't people who get bit usually turn into zombies? Kingsley would know for sure."

"In a typical story, yes." Jasper nodded. "Here, we haven't seen any bites that haven't ended in the immediate death of the individual, so I really can't say for sure. In any event, any pathogen that may have been introduced will have to go through your immune system before it kills you. If you don't mind, I think I have just the thing."

"What's that?" Harold frowned. "Something good?"

"I think so." Jasper pulled a small tube out of his pocket and started applying an ointment to Harold's wound. "It serves as a destabilizing agent when working with nitrate-based explosives, but it also works as a fantastic disinfectant. Should give your immune system a bit of help, if nothing else."

"Works for me." Harold smiled as the ointment was applied. It was soothing, that was for certain. Whether or not it was actually helping, he had no idea, but the thought was nice, at least.

Jasper soon finished, and they stood up and started walking back to the staircase. Harold frowned as they stepped into the stairwell.

"Why'd you come back for me?"

Jasper shrugged. "We were on the roof waiting, and you weren't showing up. All schools have horror stories pertaining to their basements, and I figured that it wouldn't hurt to back you up just in case one or two of them were accurate."

"Works for me." Harold nodded. "Thanks."

"Anytime." Jasper sighed as they reached the upper level. "Ready for this?"

"Not on your life." Harold chuckled. "Let's move."

They stepped out onto the roof, and Aaron spun to face them. His face lit up with relief, and he patted Jasper on the shoulder.

"We were getting worried."

"Nothing to worry about." Jasper shrugged. "Just a little scuffle with a former student."

"Uh, huh." Aaron frowned. "Well, if you two are done playing, I'd say we have work to do. You guys ready?"

"Ready as we're going to be." Jasper nodded. "You guys have your bottles of flame?"

"That we do." Frank walked over, holding a two-liter bottle of flame fluid awkwardly. "Just how am I supposed to use this thing?"

"Hold a lighter up to the end." Jasper shrugged. "There are tiny holes in the caps. The fluid builds up pressure, the cap serves as a nozzle, and you get a spurt of flame. Just don't drop it or anything. You'd probably be turned to ash in an instant."

"Why am I here anyway?" Frank muttered. "I thought I was supposed to be watching the security cameras and Garmund was supposed to be up here."

Aaron ran his hand through his hair and glanced at Harold. "I have Garmund on a… Special project."

Harold frowned slightly, but shrugged the comment away. After all, he *was* the outsider on a government team. He really couldn't blame them for not giving him all their information.

Slowly, he picked up one of the bottles and a lighter. Watching Jasper create the compound had been incredible. Even trying to follow every step, and helping with most of them, he still had no real idea of how they had managed to make so much fuel.

"How you manage to pull so much out of your hindquarters, I'll never know." Aaron muttered. "Alright, places, everyone! The goal here is to hit the church. No matter what, make sure that *someone* gets inside. If you're that someone, don't wait for the rest of us. Use your radios to call in what you find inside. Everyone else, if you see someone make it inside, unless it's the only safe option, retreat afterward. We just want to know what's there, I really don't want any more of us getting killed than is strictly necessary."

Harold held up his hand. "What radio?"

"Oh, that's right." Aaron pulled a small button out of his pocket. "Garmund handed these out when you weren't here. They'll allow you to talk to the rest of the team without any major issues."

"That's always a good thing." Harold muttered. After struggling for a few moments to figure out how to attach the button, he slipped it into his shirt pocket. Hopefully, that would work.

Aaron walked up to the edge of the roof, and Harold followed. For a moment, they just looked out over the field. They could see the church, it really wasn't that far away. In between, though, rummaging through the remnants of the Smithsonian exhibit and city park, were dozens of zombies. All of them were armored, which was terrifying enough in and of itself. Several of them appeared to be growing even larger, though, a fact that made Harold's bones tingle.

"Any theories on what's causing them to grow?" Harold frowned.

"That's what we're hitting the church for." Aaron nodded. "Let's move, people!"

Without another word, they began to descend the broken fire escape. Mr. Harris nodded at them at the top, taking up guard position again. Harold frowned as they climbed down. If he wasn't mistaken, the metal was significantly more bent than the first two times he had climbed up that evening. Someone, or something, had really done a number on it.

At the bottom, half the metal platform had simply been crumpled like a wad of paper. After glancing around and seeing no zombies, Harold leapt down to the ground, holding his bottle of flame like a baby. The rest of the team followed, soon forming a small semicircle at the base of the school. Aaron nodded at them, and they started moving.

A matter of moments passed before a roar sounded through the area. Two massive, bone-plated zombies in the city park started thumping their arms on their chest, then charged the group. Bottles of flames came up, and Aaron's voice filled the air.

"Fire!"

Harold held out his bottle as best he could, pulled a lighter from his pocket, and flicked the striker. A whoosh like none other filled the air, and a thirty-foot long flame blossomed from the plastic bottle. The fire burned bright red, a vengeance that would purify all that it came in contact with.

The two zombies that were charging them ran straight into the flame. In an instant, their bone covering was stripped away, leaving them with little more than pallid skin. It took a mere moment for the skin to blacken and sluff off, and they collapsed in a burning heap mere seconds later.

"How do you shut these things off?" Aaron yelled over the roar of the fire, looking at Jasper.

"You don't." Jasper shrugged. "We have about four more minutes before the fuel runs out. I suggest we use it!"

Aaron nodded. "That would have been nice to know *before* we all started ours at the same time. Everyone! Charge!"

Harold felt a rush enter his lungs as they move forward. His flame extended in front of him like a massive sword, a beam of energy that no one dared cross. Three more of the bone-plated zombies charged them, only to be subsequently incinerated. Too bad for them, he supposed.

They were halfway across the city park, in between two Smithsonian vans, when Frank's bottle gave a spurt and ran out. He shook his head and tossed the canister to the side, drawing a large pistol instead.

Bertha's gave out a second later, and she unstrapped a large grenade launcher from her back. Harold's was next, though as he tossed the bottle to the side, it occurred to him that he had forgotten another weapon. Horror began to set in as the gravity of that thought dawned on him, and he fought to keep his breathing even. If he was caught out here, defenseless, he would only be a drain on the team. Then again, even if he was a drain on the team, he would be *alive*. If he decided to run for it, he may or may not make it.

A few moments passed, and the rest of the flames went out. Aaron drew his pistols and backed up against a large trailer. "Alright. I can still hear more, but-"

The trailer he was leaning against was suddenly thrown out of the way. It nearly flattened him, along with Harold and the rest of the team, but was fortunately high enough that it simply knocked them to the ground. Harold forced himself to his feet again, feeling an ache in his shoulder where the portable building had hit him.

Unfortunately, he was only standing for a moment before a fist the size of his torso slammed into his body, knocking him across the ground. He came up on his feet, about twenty feet away, duly impressed and horrified by the monster now facing them.

It stood well over thirty feet tall, and was completely covered in bone plating. Additionally, horns sprouted from the head and shoulders, giving a distinctly demonic look. Tentacles shot out of its palm, wrapped around Frank, and lifted him high into the air. Its jaw opened wide, ready for the kill.

In the air, Frank pulled something off his belt. Harold couldn't see what happened next, but he could see the zombie fall back, bone melting off its face like pudding. Frank fell to the ground, a scream echoing through the air as he hit.

Harold took a deep breath, glanced back and forth, and charged for the church doors. They were only one hundred feet away… Seventy-five… Fifty…

His hand was on the doorknob when tentacles wrapped around his midsection. His feet left the ground, and he was pulled backward, away from the church. He cranked his head around, watching the zombie fill his vision. A feeling of absolute loathing flooded his veins, and he shook his head.

"I've already been bitten by one of you today! Isn't that enough?"

Harold didn't have time to receive an answer as the creature opened its armored jaw wide and stuck Harold inside, head first. As his torso filled the monstrous cavern, Harold frowned. The inside of the zombie was just as decayed as the normal zombies had seemed on the outside. Rotting flesh hung in strips, severed veins dangled like cobwebs. Why couldn't these things just finish decomposing like good corpses?

Harold frowned as he suddenly got an odd sense that he was falling. Nothing seemed to change, he was still in the zombie's mouth, and yet it seemed that gravity had ceased to exist.

With a massive whump, gravity reasserted itself, and he was thrown face-first into the rotting gullet of the monster. His face filled with decayed flesh, and he struggled not to breathe for fear of inhaling any of the liquid that oozed out of the contact point. Hands latched over his legs, and he gave a kick. He was so sick of being grabbed.

"I'm trying to help you!" The voice was unfamiliar and very obviously human. Harold stopped struggling and started trying to climb backward out of the zombie's mouth. The mysterious helper began to pull harder, dragging him backward out of the monster.

The moment he was on the ground, the stranger pulled him to his feet. "Come on! We've got to move!"

Harold glance around, trying to find his team. All he could see, though, was a dead zombie and several overturned trailers. The man, who was incredibly tall and lanky, started dragging him towards the church, and Harold nodded. With a blast, they threw the doors open and ran inside. The man shut the doors behind them, and Harold took a deep breath.

"Who-hoo!" The man hooted up into the air, before sobering. "I suggest never doing that again."

"Believe me, I don't intend to." Harold chuckled. Slowly, he took a deep breath and glanced around.

They were standing in the small vestibule of the church, a tiny entryway with few options for exit. A set of double doors led to the sanctuary, while another door led to the priest's office. The third door, one that led to the stairwell, was where the man seemed eager to move to.

"Come on, we need to get out of the entryway. They could hear us."

"You're the one that was yelling." Harold sighed and stepped into the stairway, trying to choose his words carefully. If the team was right, he was standing in Dr. Incacheck's lair. For all he knew, he was talking to the doctor himself. "So, you new in town? Come in for the exhibit?"

"I wouldn't have missed it." The man chuckled. "I drove all the way from Washington for it."

"The state?" Harold frowned. "That's quite a trek."

"No, the capital." The man frowned. "I enjoy visiting the Smithsonian a great deal. When I found out that part of it was going to be on display here, I simply had to come."

"You haven't already seen it up there?" Harold raised an eyebrow.

"Most of the Smithsonian's outreach programs, like this here, include items and exhibits that aren't usually on display." The man shrugged. "I enjoy seeing as much as possible, you know?"

"I guess." Harold nodded as they reached the basement. He hesitated before turning the knob. "So, what's your name?"

"Donald." The man shrugged. "What about you?"

"Harold." Harold frowned. "So, what made you decide to hide in the church?"

"It seemed like a good fit." The man shrugged. "Look, you obviously don't trust me, so why don't you just step through the door already? You can see what I have set up, and we can talk."

Harold shrugged, opened the door, and stepped through. The basement of the church contained a large, open room with a stage, kitchen, and plenty of tables and chairs that could be deployed or stored as they were needed. It was typically used for potlucks after mass on Sundays, though it had also been the site of many a charity dance.

Now, though, its purpose seemed entirely changed. A massive device sat in the center of the room, humming and pulsing with a thousand lights and indicators. It was shaped roughly like a cylinder, with wires and cables running up and down the entire apparatus. A small dish sat on the very top, which sparked and glowed with electricity.

The stage was also significantly altered. Makeshift cages had been set up, and half a dozen people were sitting inside the bars. One of them jumped up and started banging on the metal bars as soon as they walked inside.

The worst part, though, was the kitchen area. Laboratory equipment, including test tubes, beakers, computers, and much more that Harold couldn't even begin to decipher sat where food was usually placed for consumption. Beyond that, near the ovens, three zombies fought against a cage of their own. They seemed to be imprisoned behind a force field very similar to the one that surrounded the entire town. Harold turned to Donald, fury filling his vision.

"You're the one who did this."

"I did no such thing!" Donald's gaze turned stony. "I feel very attacked by you right now!"

"You feel attacked?" Harold growled and pointed at the cages. "How do you think *they* feel? You're nothing but a mad scientist... Incacheck."

Donald tipped his head back and laughed. "Haha! Yes, I *am* Incacheck! Bow before me or die in the zombie plague that I will use to wipe out the world!"

Harold swung his fist at Donald's head, trying to put the man out for good. Donald dodged faster than Harold would have thought possible. In an instant, Harold found his arms pinned behind his back. No matter how hard he fought, he seemed powerless to stop his capture as the doctor drug him across the room to the cages. With a rush, he unlocked the nearest cage and tossed him inside. There was only one other individual in the cell, which Harold assumed was a good thing, and Donald slammed the cage shut.

"You could have helped me." Donald gasped for breath. "It goes so much easier with help. Now, you'll just have to stay back, out of the way with the rest. You'll *die* with the rest."

"You're insane." Harold spat.

"I wouldn't be a mad scientist if I wasn't." Donald's voice almost sounded sarcastic, and Harold frowned. Interesting. Donald stared at him for a few long seconds, then slowly turned around and walked away.

Across the room, both living humans and zombies alike raged against their cells. The mad scientist, Incacheck, began to prepare dozens of chemicals. Somehow, Harold suspected that they would prove even more destructive than the stuff that Jasper could cook up.

Idly, he noticed that the doctor was mixing several chemicals into a syringe. A syringe that he was *quite* certain was meant for him. The realization set in that he might actually wind up as a zombie after all, not because of death in a fight, but because of a mad scientist and a cage.

He balled his fists and took a deep breath. If he was going to go down, he was going to go down fighting. One way or another.

CHAPTER 15

"Hey. You." Harold was drawn away from the evil scientist as the single other man in the cell yawned and sat up. "What are you in for?"

"Apparently, not helping spread evil and destruction." Harold sighed and turned away. "A group of us were trying to make it to the church. I'm the only one who got here, apparently."

"Same here." The man ran his hand through his hair and sighed. "Well, except I was the only one in my group. And I was just trying to hide. Name's Lark. I assume you're one of the locals?"

"That'd be me." Harold closed his eyes. "You come into town for the exhibit?"

"In a sense." Lark shrugged. "I'm the manager for this little operation. All I can say is that I desperately hope this gets recorded somewhere, because my boss isn't going to take a zombie attack as a valid excuse for losing the entire fleet."

"You've still got a few trailers out there." Harold held up his hands. "I think I saw two that were still standing."

"Two trailers. Out of fifteen, all of which contain priceless antiques." Lark sighed. "They're never going to let me do this again. I blew it. Of course, that's assuming that the zombies don't overtake the entire world in a terrible apocalypse."

"I hardly think a zombie attack can be considered your fault." Harold frowned. The man was concerned about his *job* in the middle of a zombie apocalypse? "Even if they never let you take stuff this far out again, they might-"

"But don't you see?" Lark held up his hands. "That was the whole point! I'm always stuck in that stupid office, surrounded by all those stupid..." He waved his hands vaguely. "I just wanted out. I wanted to see the world, so I convinced my bosses to let me come to central Kansas."

Harold frowned. Really? That was *all* the man cared about? "Then why not get a different job? As a trucker or something?"

"I like deskwork." Lark shrugged. "No manual labor. No one to stop you from playing video games instead of working."

Harold groaned. "If *that's* how you're going to act, you should be ashamed of yourself."

"Do tell?" Lark leaned back and crossed his arms. "Explain."

"You convinced your boss to bring the exhibit out here to Kansas." Harold crossed his arms to match.

"People have shown up from hours around to see this place. Which means that you brought people *straight* to the apocalypse!"

"I guess." Lark shrugged, uncaring. "How'd you get mixed up in this?"

"I live here." Harold frowned. Hadn't he *just* told Lark that? "The dead started rising, and I decided that I wanted to fight them rather than just hide."

"I see." Lark yawned. "Do you want to get out of here?"

"Believe me, I would love to." Harold glared down at Lark. What was the man driving at? "The problem is that there's a force field around the town. I think it's the same thing those zombies over there are restrained with."

"He's trying to trap the population to experiment on them." Lark frowned. "Ingenious. Annoying, but ingenious. Shoot, here he comes! Pretend we weren't talking about escaping. My suggestion, go with what he gives you. If you fight it, you wind up getting something a whole lot worse. Though..." He frowned. "If you feel yourself starting to turn, yell at me. I want ample time to kill you before you kill me."

Harold groaned and turned to face the cell door. Donald walked up to the bars a moment later, syringe in his hand. He fixed his gaze on Harold, a dark frown on his face.

"Hold out your arm, now. Or die."

"If I hold out my arm, I probably *will* die." Harold lifted an eyebrow.

"No!" Donald shrieked. "You don't get to defy my orders!"

"Pretty sure that's exactly what I'm doing." Harold shrugged and crossed his arms. "Whatever you're doing to these people, I'm not going to be a part of it."

"You're a fool." Donald spat. "You people don't realize the genius of what's happening here! The genius that *I've* engineered. If a few people have to die, millions more will live!"

"What I realize is that you turned an entire town into zombiebait." Harold leveled his gaze at the doctor. "You've killed hundreds of people tonight. Just how many are you going to kill in the long run? Thousands? Millions? Billions?"

"If I can succeed with this experiment, it could save countless more people." Donald growled. "I'll be a hero! My name will be sung along with the great individuals of this world, alongside Newton and Aponishan."

"First off, I have no idea who Aponishan is." Harold shook his head. "Second-"

"You don't know who Aponishan is?" Donald nearly exploded. His face turned red, before he sighed and ran his hand through his hair, nearly pricking himself with his needle. "No, I suppose you wouldn't. It's a secret."

"Then how… Nevermind." Harold shook his head. "*Secondly*, you can't save us by turning us into rotting corpses." He frowned after a moment. "Unless you're making us immortal? You're trying to transform the human race into something better, something evolved?"

"The best way to study the effects of rapid evolution is to use a populace that's already dead." Donald grinned and started cackling. "The cells can withstand more stress. So yes, I'm going to *help* the human race by destroying a single small town. You, since you managed to get into my lair, get to be an advanced test subject that might even be able to…" His voice trailed off, and he frowned at Harold's shoulder. "Were you bit?"

Harold took a deep breath before answering. He didn't want to answer, not in the slightest. And yet, if the doctor thought that he had *already* been infected, maybe he wouldn't bother to kill him outright? "Yeah, I guess I was bitten. Afraid I might turn into a monster and eat you?"

"No, actually. You *should* have died long before now." Donald leaned forward, frowning through the bars. "It looks like it healed incredibly well. Did you take anything for it? A disinfectant, perhaps? Have you eaten anything spicy today? Tell me! I need to know why you're not dead!"

"If you think for a single moment that I'm going to help you with your research, you've got another thing coming." Harold glared at Donald.

"Fine, then." Donald clasped his hands behind his back. The madness faded from his eyes, a stark transformation that left Harold's head spinning. "Let me put it this way. I finish my research, and I make all this go away. Maybe some more people die before I finish, as the undead outside continue to evolve and grow. Maybe they're smart enough to avoid death. That's their own problem now. If I get the results I need, I can kill every zombie in this place. That's a guarantee.

"Now, I can *also* guarantee that if I don't finish my research, your friends out there are going to continue to face a world of pain and hurt. They'll continue to fight as the zombies grow stronger and stronger, until they simply can't fight anymore. Eventually, everywhere in this city will be overrun, and the monsters will invade the church. Then… Well, then, you die."

"With any amount of luck, you'll die with us." Harold locked his jaw.

Donald held his gaze for a moment longer before bursting out in laughter, turning, and stalking away. Harold just shook his head and sat down next to Lark, who had an odd frown on his face.

"Penny for your thoughts?" Harold frowned. "You look like you just discovered something."

"Nope." Lark shook his head. "Just trying to figure out what the odds are that we can disable that machine, make it to the Smithsonian vans, and get out of town before he fixes the machine."

"Probably pretty long." Harold shrugged. "Then again, if we had a bit of help, maybe we could pull something off."

"Your team?" Lark chuckled. "Please tell me you have a comm system."

Harold frowned. Something rose in his mind… He had been given something! Slowly, he reached into his pocket and withdrew a small button. "Yeah. Yeah, I guess I do!"

"Good." Lark nodded. "Let's start talking."

CHAPTER 15

"And you *did* see Harold make it into the church?" Aaron frowned as they climbed back up the ladder. "There was no mistaking it?"

"Not a chance." Bertha nodded. "He was half-eaten by that monster that grabbed Frank, then some guy came running out of the church, killed it, and pulled him inside."

"Man, that kid has the worst luck with zombies." Jasper shook his head. "What now, boss?"

"We have to wait for him to call in." Aaron shrugged and crawled onto the roof. "Then, we'll know a bit more about what we're facing in there."

"I just hope he's okay." Jasper frowned, looking out across the lawn. "I'd hate to see anything happen to him."

"Someone has feelings for the kid." Bertha grinned and punched Jasper in the arm. "A little bit of pseudo-parent syndrome coming up?"

"I wouldn't go that far." Jasper shrugged. "He's just a good kid. I like him."

"I just hope he can get us something good." Aaron muttered. "If the button gets found by Incacheck-"

"He'll probably be killed." Jasper crossed his arms angrily. "You know, every time I think you're starting to come around, you find some way to remind me that you really don't care about this cause. Sure, you want to be the kid's hero, but you don't have a clue what that means."

Aaron sighed and put his head in his hands. "Look, this has been a long night, and-"

"It's a long night for all of us." Jasper exploded. "Harold is still going strong, if you haven't noticed. Shoot, Harold is probably doing more than all of us combined! How does that make you feel?"

"Like I need a nap." Aaron shook his head. "My vision is starting to blur, and I can barely think straight. He's doing an incredible job, there's no doubt about that."

"And you don't care about him." Jasper crossed his arms. "Not one bit. You're not concerned that he just ran into a lair of a mad scientist who was probably responsible for this whole event in the first place."

"He volunteered." Aaron met Jasper's gaze. "I can't control him. He chose to help us, and-"

"Look, I'm with Jasper on this one." Frank stepped up. "We have to care about the people we're helping, otherwise... Well, why are we doing it?"

"We're trying to stay alive." Aaron growled. "I thought that's why we were doing all of this."

"What's gotten into you?" Jasper narrowed his eyes and stepped up to Aaron's face. "One minute you're all gung-ho about rescuing people, the next moment, you're more than ready to throw in the towel and let everyone else do your work for you. Where's the consistency?"

"You know what?" Aaron threw his hands up. "I don't know. I don't know!" A roar echoed his yells in the distance, and Aaron lowered his voice. "Right now, I don't know what I want. All I know is that my body hurts, my emotions are out of whack, and I just want to sleep. Part of me wants to charge back to the church to make sure he's okay. Part of me just wants to give it all up. You know, I'm really not good about-"

"Guys?" Harold's voice echoed in Aaron's ear. "Can you hear me?"

Aaron put his finger to his ear, pressing the *talk* button on the earpiece. "Yeah, we can hear you."

"Guys?" Harold's voice repeated. "Can you hear me? This thing must be broken."

"He doesn't have it in his ear." Jasper's head dropped. "He's probably just talking to it."

"Harold!" Frank yelled at the top of his lungs. "Put this in your ear!"

"What was that?" Harold's voice sounded confused. "I heard…"

There was a burst of static from the earpiece, and a new voice came on. "Hey, there. Name's Lark. Harold was having problems figuring out how to work the comm system."

"Good to know." Aaron muttered. "What's the situation in-"

Another burst of static cut in, and Harold's voice reappeared a moment later. "Alright, got this thing back. You guys hear me now?"

"Loud and clear." Aaron sighed.

"Wow!" Harold's voice sounded excited. "This thing is incredible!"

"You can marvel about it later." Aaron muttered. "What can you tell about what's happening in there?"

"Well, your Incacheck is here." Harold's voice quieted a good bit. "He has a big machine that I assume is the force field generator, a bunch of zombies that he has trapped in a bunch of other force fields, and a bunch of humans that he's been running experiments on."

"Experiments how?" Aaron frowned. "Any details?"

There was a pause, and Harold's voice came back on. "He's been injecting them with something. No one really knows what. So far, nothing has seemed to happen, but he's been walking past the cage with a scanner every so often. He's pretty intent on what he's doing. He told me that this whole thing is to try and evolve the population of the entire world. Your guess is as good as mine what they actually mean."

"Great." Aaron paused. "I'm assuming you're trapped?"

"Isn't that obvious?" Harold's voice was sarcastic. "Yeah, I'm trapped. I'm in a cage with Lark here, he thinks he might have an idea to escape."

"Really?" Aaron perked up at that. "I'm all ears. What's the plan?"

"He worked with the Smithsonian exhibit. If you notice, the only things you see in the city park are trailers, not the actual vans used to pull the trailers."

Aaron nodded. "He knows where the vans themselves are."

"Bingo." Harold took a deep breath. "They're stored over in a field on the south side of town. If we can make it there, we can probably get away."

"Force field, remember?" Aaron muttered. "Kind of puts a damper on it all."

"If we can damage the force-field generator in here before we leave, we can knock it down for long enough to get out." Harold's voice sounded confident. "Granted, that also lets a bunch of zombies loose on the population, but one thing at a time, right?"

Aaron turned to Jasper. "You two put a bunch of explosives in the basement, right?"

"That we did." Jasper nodded. "Enough to send the school to mars, I think."

Aaron nodded. "Garmund? You on here?"

"Here." Garmund's voice came on the line. "What's up?"

"How many zombies left in the city?" Aaron closed his eyes as he tried to think. "Any fewer?"

"The zombie population is down to about ninety." Garmund's voice sounded grim. "That group out at the diner is taking care of a lot of them. Seems like they got their hands on some military tech of some sort. You want me to send you their positions?"

"I want the positions of the zombies." Aaron nodded slowly as a plan formulated in his mind. "We have to kill each and every one of them before we leave."

There was a short silence.

"You're going to do what?" Bertha spoke into the silence. "I thought we decided a few moments ago that you were past the point of caring."

"I don't know what I want, alright!" Aaron screamed into the sky. "What I know is that if we leave even one zombie alive, they'll escape into the world, and this process starts all over again. We face this problem again in a few months, just against a world of the creatures rather than ninety. Now, where are they most clustered and what have they evolved into?"

"It looks like there are about thirty zombies in close proximity to the city park." Garmund's voice was thoughtful. "About fifty are trying to break through the diner line, but since they haven't evolved very far, the diner is holding them back pretty well. The rest are scattered around... Oh."

"I don't like *ohs*." Aaron muttered. "What's up now?"

"The zombies throughout town are starting to converge on the church." Garmund's voice was tight. "Maybe they realized that they can't evolve without being near the building?"

"Or something that's controlling them is trying to level them up as fast as possible." Aaron sighed and brushed his hair out of his eyes. "Harold? Get out of there as fast as you can. See what you can do to damage the shields on your way, but just get out of there."

"You do realize that I'm trapped, right?" Harold's voice was tight. "Any great ideas?"

"I've got a few." Jasper's voice came on. "Follow these instructions, and follow them carefully."

As Jasper started talking chemistry, Aaron tuned them out and turned to the rest of the group.

"Alright, we need to get those vans, and we need to get them quickly. Once we have them, half of us goes to the diner to pick up that group, the rest comes back here to the school. We load up everyone from the school while simultaneously luring the rest of the zombies into the building. As soon as they're there, we blow the bomb, wiping all the creatures from the town. Sound like a plan?"

"And we're going to fit two hundred people into three vans?" Bertha growled. "Sounds like a plan that's going to get us killed."

"I think the good doctor has a pretty good plan that will also get us killed." Aaron muttered. "Harold? How many vans does the exhibit have?"

"Hang on, I'm trying to make an acid."

"We don't have time for-"

"Seven. They brought seven vans."

"So we're going to fit two hundred people into-"

"We'll figure it out." Aaron cut off the argument. "Frank, go down and relieve Garmund of his position. You're on security detail now."

"Sounds perfect." Frank nodded and vanished into the stairs.

"Good." Aaron took a quick count in his head. "That means we have myself, Bertha, Jasper, Garmund, Harold, and Lark to drive, assuming we all make it out alive. We need one more person."

"You've got me." Mr. Harris stepped out of the stairwell. "I'm done standing on this roof, running errands for his majesty. Tell me what to do."

"Run and drive." Aaron shrugged. "Oh, and shoot as many of these monsters as you can. That'll be nice, too."

"It will be my pleasure." Mr. Harris nodded grimly. "My shotgun will burn with the vengeance of those lost tonight."

"As long as zombies die, I don't rightly care what kind of poetry you can recite." Aaron sighed and turned back towards the church. "Harold? Status?"

"Still working on the acid." Harold muttered. "Be patient."

"Be patient." Aaron muttered. "That's what they all say. How in the world are you making-"

"Look, just go." Harold's voice was tight. "We'll be along as soon as we can. Should only be a minute or two. Besides, the moment we get into the thick of things, all plans are going to go out the window."

"On it." Aaron nodded. "See you at the vans."

"See you then." Harold's voice went dead, and Aaron nodded.

"Alright, no stopping until you see the lights of the vans." He took a deep breath. "Here's to victory."

CHAPTER 17

Harold held his breath as he poured the acid onto the lock of the cage. There was a hiss as the metal dissolved, and the cage clicked loudly. Lark nodded at him, and he slid the door wide open.

The moment they stepped outside, Donald looked up from where he was dissecting a zombie arm that kept thrashing even though it wasn't attached to any particular zombie. With a rush, he charged towards the two escapees.

"You can't leave me!"

"Oh, I think we can." Harold stepped forward to meet the charge. As Donald swung a wiry fist at Harold's head, Harold slammed a fist into Donald's ribs. Donald gasped, snorted, and continued his charge.

Harold shrugged and sidestepped the attack. Donald frowned as he overextended, spun, and raised his fists again.

Harold just stood there for a few moments while a small trace amount of venom did its work. Donald's eyes opened wide as he started to sway, and he ran for his workbench. Harold did nothing to stop him, and frowned as the doctor managed to grab a bottle off a shelf and pop several pills before collapsing on the ground.

"What did you do to him?" Lark frowned. "That's not in any fighting manual I've ever seen."

"I'm not sure which is worse, the fact that you didn't see me preparing the probe, or the fact that you study fighting manuals." Harold chuckled. "Jasper talked me through creating a small amount of venom using the same stuff I used to create the acid. I just put it on a needle and stuck it in him. It'll only keep him out for a few minutes."

"So we should be moving, then." Lark gestured at the door. "Like, right now."

Harold nodded, walked over to the force field generator, and started stripping down wires. The machine began to flicker, and he grinned.

"Perfect! It should go down in a few minutes, assuming I did it right. And we have our way out."

A scream echoed through the hall, and he spun to see the three zombies imprisoned behind force fields escaping into the hall. One of them was trying to claw its way through the bars of the cages, but it didn't seem to be having much luck. Idly, Harold noticed that it didn't seem to have evolved at all. Interesting.

As one of them stumbled towards him, Harold glanced around, walked over to a game table, and grabbed a pool cue that had been used in dozens of church activities, few of which were actually pool. Without pausing, he

rammed the pool cue through the zombie's head, dropping it in an instant.

With a rush, he jogged over and stabbed the zombie threatening the cages, then stabbed the third that seemed to be getting ready to eat Dr. Incacheck. As much as he detested the man for what he had done to the town, there was no real need to let him die and come back as a zombie.

"Hey! You going to let us out?" A woman trapped in the cage held her hands out. "Please?"

Harold sighed and rubbed the back of his neck. "Honestly, you're going to be a lot safer in there than out in the streets."

"I don't care!" The woman thrashed against the bars. "Please! Let us out!"

Harold sighed, jogged over to the still-unconscious Dr. Incacheck, and started fishing through his pockets until he found a small key. In the reverse situation, he would have been begging to be let free as well, so he really couldn't blame any of them for wanting to be let loose. And if it hindered the doctor's research, then *maybe* a few deaths really would save the larger population. A few moments later, he had unlocked the rest of the cages. The captives, ten in all, blew past him without so much as a word.

Lark looked at him and shrugged. "Well, you can't win them all."

"I can't really win any." Harold muttered. "Alright, let's move. I'm done with this place."

"You fool." Dr. Incacheck muttered as he stirred and started to sit up. "You're going to kill us all."

"I thought you already had that covered." Harold spread his arms. "Now, if you'll excuse me, we're going to go save the world."

Harold and Lark left the room at a trot. They raced up the stairs and forced the church doors open. Without another word, they stepped out into absolute chaos.

Four of the zombies now stood at least thirty feet tall and were inflicting absolute destruction on the area. The captives that they had just released had scattered, and were busily being chased across the area. The woman who had begged for release made it all the way to the hardware store before the monster caught her, swept her up, and ate her in a single bite.

"Well, at least they're not turning into more zombies." Lark muttered. "Come on, we need to get moving."

With a burst of speed, Lark took off across the city park. Harold followed him, almost thankful for the distraction that the other escapees were creating. *Almost.* Before they had made it far, a massive monster noticed him and charged across the park, arms and tentacles extended.

As the massive hands closed over him, Harold dropped, allowing himself to faceplant on the grass. He had been hoping for a summersault, but the faceplant allowed the hand to pass cleanly over him. Without slowing, the monster simply altered course and went after another man who was doing his best to hide behind a tree. It took two full bites for the zombie to finish him off, but by that time, Harold was back on his feet and moving as fast as he could.

Ahead of him, Lark ducked into one of the remaining Smithsonian trailers that hadn't been flipped yet.

Harold followed him, confused, shutting the door behind him as he did so.

"Aren't we supposed to be running for the vans?" He frowned. "I thought that was the whole idea."

"It is." Lark nodded as he flicked a flashlight over several rows of artifacts behind red ropes. "I just… There's something here I need to take first."

"What artifact could possibly be worth your life?" Harold frowned.

"It's actually saving our lives." Lark hissed. "If you'll notice, nothing is trying particularly hard to kill us right now. They were too busy and didn't notice us get in here. If we hadn't hidden, there was no getting through them before they finished with their other snacks and got to us."

Harold shuddered as he pictured the deaths outside. Living because others were dying. "So what are you looking for?"

"This." Lark paused as his eyes settled on a display case. It held a single shard of stone, about three inches long and a single inch wide. A symbol was engraved on it, a half-moon with a rod bisecting it. At a glance, it almost looked like a drawn bow, though it didn't have a string with which to shoot the arrow.

"It looks like a diagram of how to hunt an animal." Harold shrugged. "Nothing major."

"It was a chip off a tablet found near the body of a Spanish Missionary who came over with Columbus." Lark smiled, broke the case open using what looked like an ancient axe, and reached inside. "There are some who speculate that the tablet was the legendary philosopher's stone, and that the missionary came over to America to try and hide it from the sorcerers of England that were trying to use it for their own ends."

Harold chuckled. "You believe in the philosopher's stone?"

Lark shrugged. "Let's just say that I don't like to discount theories until they're proven false." Slowly, he picked up a cloth next to the shard, wrapped it in the cloth without ever letting it touch his skin, and dropped it into his pocket. "Call me what you will, but this thing has long since fascinated me." He grinned. "Now, I can add it to my own, personal collection. No more having to see it in a museum display case, I can have it whenever I want. We can go now."

"Finally." Harold muttered. The curator was stealing from his own collection. What an *upstanding* character. "Now, any good ideas for how we get from the trailer to the vans now that the zombies have finished up everyone else?"

"Actually, I do." Lark walked to the front of the trailer, where he pulled a small key from his pocket and unlocked a large case. "Knock yourself out."

Harold walked up to the case, and his jaw dropped. Inside were dozens of weapons, ranging from a small machine gun to several grenades.

"What in tarnation does the Smithsonian need with this kind of weaponry?"

"There are always threats against Smithsonian goods." Lark shrugged. "In the past, they've actually been attacked by all manners of terrorist groups, even private collectors with deep pockets."

Harold nodded and picked up the machine gun. "I don't know if it'll do any good, but it looks fun."

"In that case, let's move out." Lark grinned. "Vans, here we come!"

With a burst of speed, they tore out the back of the van, racing across the turf as fast as they could. One of the largest monsters, directly in front of them, spun and started racing towards them. Lark pulled the pin on a grenade and lobbed it into the creature's mouth as it bent down. It exploded quite spectacularly, and Harold rushed past in a blur.

Ahead of them, several of the original bone-crusted zombies lurched out of the dark. It was almost a relief to see zombies less than ten feet tall, and Harold cut loose with his machine gun. Lark added in his own contribution with a grenade, and the night rang with the cries of fallen monsters. A slightly larger zombie charged towards Harold, and he readjusted his aim. For several long moments, he simply poured lead into the creature. He could see bone chipping off with each bullet, ever-so-slowly eating away at the creature.

It was only a matter of feet from him when he finally wore through the bone and sent its remaining brains spinning through the air. It collapsed, and he dodged out of the way. Lark nodded, and the tore out of the park.

Together, they raced past several rows of houses, grinning as the zombies scaled back to simple runners. Lark pulled out a pistol and started shooting, downing monster after monster. Harold fired a few bursts with his weapon, but held out mostly to conserve ammo. They fought their way to the south side of town as one being, mowing down everything that came their way.

Several long minutes later, they finally arrived at the field. The white vans loomed out of the darkness, and several clicks filled the air as they stepped up.

"What took you so long?" Aaron appeared around the hood of one of the vehicles.

"We stopped for drive-through." Harold muttered. "We had to go through that crowd of three-story creatures! You wouldn't have been moving that quickly, either."

"Well, you're late." Aaron put his hand up to his ear. "What's the zombie count?"

"Less than fifty." Frank's voice grated in Harold's ear. "Assuming, of course, that these readings are correct. About thirty at the diner, twenty more in the park. Those twenty are a doozy, though."

"Lock and load, then." Aaron nodded. "Harold, Lark, Bertha, I want you to hit the diner. Clear out the zombies, get everyone on board, and head for the hills. I don't want to see your faces again until we meet somewhere else."

"Where are we meeting?" Harold frowned. "Anywhere close?"

"Not if I have anything to say about it." Aaron muttered. "For the moment, plan on meeting in Garden City. We can drop off all the refugees, then make our way back to Kansas City from there. Incidentally, you're welcome to come with us if you want to. These comm systems aren't going to work unless we're less than half a mile apart, which means that we won't have communication with each other after we leave. I can't stress enough how-"

"Yeah, yeah, yeah. Make sure we get our parts done." Bertha waved her hand. "We've got it. If either group fails, we're letting a swarm of evil out into the world."

"Actually, I was going to say that we don't get our jobs back, but hey, that works too." Aaron chuckled. "Ready to-"

"Wait, what?" Harold frowned. "What do you mean, get your jobs back? I thought this *was* your job."

The silence that ensued seemed to stretch into eternity. Harold's eyes narrowed. "Are you *not* the Apocalypse Squad?"

CHAPTER 18

Aaron sighed. "It's complicated."

"No, I really don't think it is." Harold crossed his arms. "Either you are who you say you are, or you aren't."

Aaron's head fell. "We didn't lie about a thing. We're from the Apocalypse Prevention Department, though we haven't really gone by 'Apocalypse Squad' before tonight."

"Okay." Harold crossed his arms. "What aren't you telling me?"

"That's really not the point here."

"It had better be the point." Harold crossed his arms. "I put my life in your hands. I let you save me, over and over, and now I find out that you're not who you say you are. Well, right now, we're going into a major battle. I need to know who I'm working with!"

Aaron took a deep breath and looked up at the sky. "We're the misfits of the government. No other event like this has ever happened in recorded history. We were thrown into this department because that's what the government figured would be the easiest way to dispose of us."

Harold's eyes pierced even more. "Why are you *here*, then?"

Aaron ran his hand through his beard. "We were told that unless we actually did our job, saved the world, we were going to be kicked out onto the street, incarcerated, or executed. None of us really liked those options, so…"

"So you came out here because you wanted to keep your cushy government seat." Harold's gaze was firey.

Bertha held up her hand. "Actually, we came out here to try and fake an apocalypse so they could see that we were trying. We really weren't expecting any of this, know what I mean?"

"It means you're all frauds." Harold took a step back. "You're not worthy of saving this town."

"Maybe they aren't." Lark held up his hand. "That said, the way I see it, they're our only hope, misfits or not. They have the most firepower, and they have a workable plan to escape. The way I see it, the best thing you can do is help them out and rat them out to the government later."

Harold took a deep breath. "I hate this."

"We're not exactly thrilled to be here, either." Jasper stepped forward. "Look, none of us were prepared for this. The important thing to remember is that we fought together, worked as one to defeat this threat. You already took down Incacheck, which should award you a decent reward from the government in and of itself. Stick with us a little longer, a few more hours, and you'll be free."

Harold shook his head before finally nodding. "Fine. I'll stick with you. Let's just get this over with."

"Fine by me." Aaron walked to the nearest van, opened the door, and climbed inside. "Move out!"

CHAPTER 19

Harold climbed in his van, a feeling of betrayal flooding his system. He had *trusted* these people! He knew Lark was right, they were his best option, but what else could he feel? They had told him that they came to help the situation, when they had only come to help themselves. Typical government.

He sat his machine gun on the seat next to him, fired up the vehicle, and took a deep breath. If he was right, the group was in the Home and Deli bar and diner. He was the only one who knew the way, which meant that he got to go first.

After waiting a moment to make sure that the rest of the group was in their vehicles, he pressed down on the accelerator and tore out from the grass. His wheels hit the asphalt, and he ripped into town. A stumbling zombie walked out into the street, and he drove straight over it, feeling little more than a dull thump from the impact. He only wished it could have been one of the squad instead of a faceless monster.

After a moment of thought, he spun onto a side street, primarily so he wouldn't have to go past the city park again. This street would loop around the edge of town, come out on the highway that led to Garden City, which would allow him to get right up next to the diner.

His wheels spun on the gravel, and for a moment, he nearly skidded off the road and into a house. Fortunately, a lifetime of road racing allowed him to ride out the skid and stay on track, sending him down the road at quite a clip.

The road began to curve around the edge of town, and he grinned as he tore around the bend. Perfect. All that had to do was stay alive.

Ahead, blotting out the stars, a monstrous zombie loomed on the road. It turned towards him, and he took a deep breath. Great. If he had had someone riding shotgun, they at least could have started using his machine gun, but as it was, he was pretty much helpless.

With nothing else to do, he spun onto another side road, this one heading out of town. A dull thud echoed through the air to indicate that they were being chased, and he groaned. Why couldn't they just leave him alone?

If he was right, he could take the road out of town, turn on a field road immediately past the last row of houses, and still meet the highway. He just hoped that he wouldn't slow down enough for the creature to catch him. Slowly, he took a deep breath as the turn neared. This was it.

With gut-wrenching force, he tore around the bend. The wheels of his van lifted off the road, and he grimaced. He was so close. All he needed was…

A hand slammed into the side of the van, and it went flying. The word spun outside his window, and the world grew even darker than it had been. When the vehicle came to a stop, metal slammed into his body as the door was dented inward, and he groaned. The van was quite obviously never running again, at least not without substantial mechanical work. A massive foot slammed into the ground just in front of him, before vanishing as the monster ran off.

Another van pulled up next to him, and he threw the door open. It took him a moment to grab his weapon, and he bailed out. The zombie, well over thirty feet tall, pounded down the road only feet away, chasing after another set of lights. The passenger door clicked open for him, and he dove inside. Wheels spun, and they were off.

"The thing is chasing Lark." Bertha grimaced. "Does he know where to go?"

"I sure hope so." Harold muttered as he shifted the weapon on his lap. Idly, he scooted as far away from the woman as he could. "He mentioned spending time around town the last few days, so there's a chance."

In front of them, Lark's headlights spun to the left, and Harold nodded as the massive creature turned to follow. "He's heading the right direction. We'll see what happens next."

"That we will." Bertha grimaced. "Alright, as soon as we get around this corner, I want you to start shooting. See if you can draw him away, and we'll try to take him out once we can get our weapons out."

"You guys have the worst plans ever." Harold muttered.

"Our original plan was to blow up a town and blame it on Incacheck." Bertha shrugged. "As far as plans go, I'm not too concerned about this one."

Harold turned and scowled at her. Why would she *admit* to that? Why...

"Dealing with a situation here." Bertha snapped.

"Take care of your own problems." Harold frowned at her, and she gestured vaguely at her head. "Aren't you listening to the coms?"

"Been a bit busy for that." Harold sighed.

They spun around the corner, lined up with the road, and took off again. Harold picked up his machine gun, propped it up on the dashboard, and took a deep breath. He set the zombie's head in his sights, staring down the barrel at the bone-crusted creature. The diner was only a few hundred feet away, and they were leading a gigantic monster *straight* towards it. What saviors they were.

Before he could pull the trigger, a trail of flame launched upward from the roof of the diner. It struck the monster in the face, blowing its head off in a glorious explosion. The creature collapsed, Bertha spun the wheel as she dodged around the corpse of the creature, and Harold shook his head.

"What in creation just happened?"

"I'm hoping we find out." Bertha shrugged. "Here's the diner. Ready to play?"

Harold nodded and readjusted his weapon. Bertha spun into the parking lot of the Home and Deli, where dozens of zombies were lined up against the windows, pounding uselessly on the glass. They turned as the vehicles came roaring in, and Harold stepped out onto the gravel.

With a roar, he cut loose with his machine gun. Bullets flew through the air, mowing down the creatures as fast as they could come. Glass shattered behind them, ripping into the store itself. He smiled grimly as he cut down each and every monster in the lot. Oh, it was nice to actually be able to do damage to the creatures.

"Any more in my area?" He held his finger up to the com in his ear. "Or did I get them all?"

"There's one right behind you." Frank's voice echoed through his ear. "I'd move if I was you."

Harold leapt forward as a rotting hand scraped across his shoulder. He spun to see a creature lurching towards him, so close there was no possible way for him to get his weapon raised in time. Was this it? Was…

With a dull splat, a chopstick was driven through the zombie's head, coming out between its eyes. The creature dropped, revealing Bertha standing just behind the monster holding a box of moldy Chinese takeout. At Harold's incredulous look, she shrugged.

"I shoved all the trash under the seat instead of actually cleaning it out. Less work than hauling it all the way to the dumpster."

Harold snorted. "I thought you were the grenade launcher girl."

"Guys are always concerned with how big things are." She glanced down at the fallen corpse. "Sometimes I just like things to be precise."

Harold shrugged, and turned back to the diner as a man stepped through the ruins of the front window. He was from out of town, likely someone that had been eating supper at the diner when everything went south.

"You our rescue?"

"That would be me." Harold nodded. "It'll be crowded, but we need everyone to cram into these two vans."

"There are few enough of us left that that shouldn't be an issue." The man waved his arms, and about twenty people came through the desolation. "I hope how we handled that monster was okay."

"Honestly, I'm just curious how you managed to get your hands on that kind of explosives." Harold shrugged. "I thought it was pretty impressive."

"Well, we're officially out now, so I'm all for escaping." The man waited until the vans were filled, then nodded at Harold. "After you."

Harold patted his gun. "I'm in shotgun. Makes things easier if it gets nasty."

"Fair enough." The man nodded.

A moment later, Harold was crammed into the seat, practically sitting on the man's lap, as the vans roared out of town. With a flicker, the force field overhead lit up, blocking out the stars with a blinding light, then vanished.

Harold winced as they reached they came within sight of a number of wrecked vehicles sitting on the road. If the force field wasn't down…

With a breathtaking blur, they tore past the wrecks and continued out of town. They were heading north, out of desolation, toward humanity again. He rolled down the window and sucked in a deep breath of air as the first rays of light crested the horizon. He had survived the night! For the first time in over twenty-four hours, he felt truly free.

Whatever happened next, he was certain that the worst was behind him.

CHAPTER 20

Aaron put the vehicle in gear, feeling the power beneath the hood of the van. Granted, it wasn't a ton of power. In fact, most motorcycles probably had higher engine outputs. That said, it still felt nice to be driving *something*. They were heading into the final showdown. This was it.

Harold roared off in a spray of dirt, vanishing into the darkness. Aaron took a deep breath as Frank's voice sounded in his ear.

"Okay, looks like the diner crew is en route. Oh."

"I don't like that kind of talk." Aaron muttered. "What's wrong?"

"They ran into one of those skyscraper zombies." Frank's voice was even. "Looks like they're giving it quite a chase, though."

"That's something." Aaron sighed and brushed his hair to the side. "Alright, we're moving. Stay tight, and get ready to move. You'll have to be out of there with everyone else."

"I'll stay until I absolutely have to leave." Frank's voice was temporarily drowned out as Aaron floored the vehicle. "That way you guys have me for the longest-"

"Got to let you go." Aaron yelled over the roar of the engine, which sounded entirely too loud. "See you on the other side!"

With that, Aaron sent the vehicle diving onto the asphalt road into town. All they had to do was get to the school, get everyone out, and lure the zombies in. No biggie, right?

As the flew past the city park, a roar sounded above even the scream of the engine. Aaron frowned and glanced to the side, where at least five of the behemoths stood in the city park, ready to kill. They began to run in his direction, charging across the distance in leaps and bounds. Tentacles stretched out from their palms, enhancing their already-extreme reach.

"Change of plan!" Aaron yelled into his microphone. "Frank, get everyone out! There's no way we can load the vans before they're on us. We'll distract them for a few minutes, then get them into the school."

"Where do I take everyone?" Frank's voice sounded panicked. "What do I do?"

"Tell the principle that he needs to take everyone north!" Aaron took a deep breath. "That will be away from the bulk of the zombies. Once that's done, I need a headcount on the remaining zombies."

"On it." Frank's voice went silent, and Aaron desperately hoped that everyone else was listening to the com system.

"If you didn't hear the new plan, just stay on my tail! We have to keep them busy!"

"I'm sick of being the bait." Garmund's voice drifted through his ear. "Can't we make Bertha be the bait instead?"

"Dealing with a situation here." Bertha's voice snapped. "Take care of your own problems."

"Jasper!" Aaron yelled as he threw the van into a sharp corner. "Any good weapons on you?"

"I could make a decent bomb out of the gasoline, but I've got jack on me right now."

"Great." Aaron tapped his fingers against the steering wheel, before a thought struck him. "Jasper! Where did you drop that big gun of yours?"

"The electrophotometer? I can't describe the location, but I can get there."

"Do it." Aaron gasped as he took another corner substantially sharper than he probably should have. The church blazed past him, allowing him to see a stunned-looking scientist standing on the front steps. "Oh, and it looks like Incacheck is back on his feet."

"That's not the news I want to hear right now." Garmund's voice was tight. "Hey, I couldn't get my car around that corner. I'm on a different street now."

"Stay ahead of the thing." Aaron yelled back. "And try to hang to the south. We don't want to interfere with the people escaping the school."

"Doing my best."

An explosion echoed through the night, and Aaron jumped as he threw the car into another tight corner. "Anyone know what that was?"

"Looked to me like they managed to take down one of those big ones over on the other side of town." Mr. Harris's voice came through the system. "Couldn't tell you any details. Saw the silhouette in the fire."

"That's something." Aaron muttered. "Is anyone still on my tail?"

"I'm trying." Mr. Harris gasped. "You're not making it easy. This thing's awfully close to me. You've got one on your right."

Aaron spun around a corner to his left, a loud scrape echoing through the vehicle as a hand scraped down the right side of the van.

"Thanks."

"Not a problem." Mr. Harris sighed deeply. "It's falling back. Wait."

A loud crash echoed through the earpiece, and Aaron felt something hit him in his gut.

"Harris?"

There was no answer, and Aaron bit his lip. "Anyone have eyes on Harris?"

"Nope." Garmund's voice was tight. "I've just got two of these things on my tail. Haven't seen anyone since I split off."

"Jasper?"

"Just picked up my gun. Haven't seen a soul for several minutes."

"Frank?"

There was a pause. "Still trying to convince the principal to get out of the building."

Aaron sighed. "Pull a gun on him if you have to! Just get him out of there!"

There was a several second pause, during which Aaron tore past a number of houses, turned onto a side road, and found himself in the same field that they had started in. Without further ado, he flew back into town, glancing around for anyone.

"Guys? Meet in the city park." Jasper's voice sounded like he had been running. "Bring as much company as possible."

"I'll do my best." Aaron caught a glimpse of something in the darkness, and spun his vehicle in that direction. At least ten of the basic armored creatures stormed out of an alley, crashing into the vehicle before he had a chance to do anything. With nothing else to do, Aaron simply plowed forward, shoving them to the side as he pulled through onto another street.

"Alright, I see one… I see two…"

"I'm almost there." Aaron gasped. "Don't start without me."

"Don't worry." Jasper's voice was tight. "After we entertain the guests you're bringing, head to my position. We've got enough supplies for an entire rave."

Aaron didn't bother to respond, as he blew out of a side street and onto the city park. Another van ripped around the outside of the park, chased by three behemoths. A light flashed in the center of the park, and Aaron floored it across the grass, ready to cross its path.

The other van, presumably driven by Garmund, flipped onto the grass and flew by in the opposite direction. They crossed almost perfectly in front of a wide-open trailer. The hoard behind Aaron came into alignment with the monsters chasing Garmund, and with a blast of light, streamers exploded from the back of the trailer.

The air seemed to bend, and Aaron felt static electricity pop up and down his body. With a rush, he slammed on his brakes and felt the van skid to a halt. About fifty feet from the back of the trailer, he bailed out, turned, and ran back towards Jasper's position as quickly as he could.

The zombies that had been chasing them were gone, transformed to ash. Jasper pointed his gun up at the sky, launching ribbons of energy towards the heavens, creating a beacon of energy for anyone who dared look. As Aaron ran up, he saw a grin plastered over Jasper's face.

"You're having entirely too much fun with this."

"Well, get ready to have a whole lot more." Jasper chuckled as Garmund appeared. "If I'm right, that should have attracted pretty much the rest of the town."

Roars sounded in the night, and shadows began to move. Jasper dropped the drained weapon and picked up a machine gun.

"It's not modified by yours truly, but it's a start."

"Where's mine?" Aaron held out his hands. Jasper gestured behind him, and Aaron glanced past him to see a pile of weapons that could have come from a military compound.

"It was meant to guard this stuff." Jasper shrugged. "I figured this was a suitable use."

"I concur." Aaron nodded. He picked up a weapon and turned, back against the trailer. "Here they come."

Garmund grabbed his own weapon, and the battle was on. Dozens of the creatures seemed to appear out of the night, charging towards their positions. They ranged from the simple armored creatures to the massive behemoths. After a few of them, the trio learned to work together, concentrating their fire on the larger ones to drop them faster.

Aaron's arms were beginning to grow numb when the last visible zombie dropped. Frank's voice echoed through their headsets, a welcome sound.

"Looks like there's only one left. He's… Oh."

"How many times do-" Aaron's voice trailed off as the stars began to blink out in front of him. "Oh."

The zombie was visibly growing in front of them, rising higher and higher into the night. Forty feet… Fifty feet… Seventy feet… Light began to glow from the mass, giving some illumination in the darkness. Fire seemed to blossom under its skin, spikes ripped from its skull, enormous tentacles dropped from its arms, and a bellowing roar nearly deafened Aaron's fragile eardrums.

"Any ideas?" Aaron glanced at Jasper. "I don't see any way we take this thing down!"

"Use the drones." Garmund put his finger to his ear. "Frank! Hit it with the drones!"

"Where are its controls?" Frank's voice sounded confused. "Is it-"

Something whistled over Aaron's head, and a nearby trailer exploded with brilliant light.

"Wrong button!" Garmund yelled. "Alright, stop. Do you see the little blue button in the corner?"

"Yeah."

"Push it."

"Got it." Frank's voice seemed to light up. "Say, that's handy."

"Yeah." Garmund sounded relieved. "It's an automatic threat tracking system. Just touch the big red demon on the screen and we'll-"

A resounding boom sounded through the night as fire blossomed on the monster's shoulder. It roared in challenge, only to be instantly drowned out by a blast of fire coming from seven drones exploding at once. Aaron saw its head snapped backward, and the monster collapsed. It landed on the church, flattening the steeple in one fell swoop.

For a few moments, no one dared breathe. Aaron finally barked a laugh, a chuckle that failed to stop, no matter how hard he tried. After several long moments, he sucked in a deep breath and tried to keep his composure together.

"Any more of them?"

"Don't think so." Frank's voice was quiet. "All my cameras are dead, so I don't know that for certain, but it sure seems that way."

"Then we're calling it a night." Aaron nodded as the shield overhead flickered and died. "I'm climbing in my van. Have everyone at the front of the school in five minutes. We're getting out of here."

As Aaron climbed into the vehicle, he glanced over at the church. For a moment, he thought he saw something move in the entrance, a brief glimmer of… Well, something. After a few seconds, he shook his head. Frank had said that there was only one more, and that was that.

He started up the van and began moving it towards the high school. A few moments later, he pulled up in front of the door, which were in the process of being wrenched open. A grin split his face as the first of the survivors swarmed out. They had made it. Somehow, they had survived.

Now, all that was left to do was go home.

CHAPTER 21

Principle Gruen stood in the locker room, mixed feelings flowing through his mind. On one hand, it was relieving to know that the zombies were gone. There was no more fear of monsters clawing through the walls of his fortress, there was no more terror involving someone trying to overthrow his reign. He was free.

On the other hand, he had rather enjoyed being in charge. It had been comforting, he supposed, to have dozens of people under his rule, doing everything he said. After all, hadn't he became a principle for that very same reason?

Slowly, knowing that he would have to bid his kingdom goodbye, he stepped into the hospital. Below the showers, those cots had seen... Well, not really that much action. In fact, their only resident ever was still there.

Kingsley, who had apparently been knocked unconscious during a zombie attack, lay on a cot just inside the door.

Principle Gruen hesitated for only a moment before picking the boy up off his cot. Nearly everyone else was evacuated, it wouldn't be right to allow the kid to potentially be forgotten. Once they got back to civilization, Kingsley might even vouch for the principle, giving him fame and fortune for how good of a leader he had been.

As he walked out of the locker room, something seemed to shift in his arms. He looked down to see something like snakes crawling around under Kingsley's skin. Startled, he dropped the boy and stepped back, equally horrified that he had just dropped a student and that there had been… something… living inside the boy.

As Kingsley hit the ground, his skin ruptured, allowing long, dark tentacles to erupt outward. Three slammed into Principle Gruen's stomach, driving through him like stakes. He was slammed back into the wall, but at that moment, he hardly cared about the impact. Tentacles flowed into his veins, and he felt the world swim away from him.

CHAPTER 22

"Almost done." Frank nodded to Aaron as he slammed the rear doors shut on his van. "I think the only ones left are Kingsley and the Principle."

"I'd be fine leaving one of the two." Aaron chuckled. "Go check on him, why don't you?"

"Why me?" Frank muttered, then frowned. "Why are we taking these people from here, anyway? Now that we killed everything-"

"Dr. Incacheck obviously planted *something* here that caused anything dead to come back to life." Aaron shrugged. "Until we can determine what that was and if the effect was taken down when the shield fell, we have to get out of here."

"Makes sense." Frank turned towards the entrance of the school, blanched, and turned back. "On second thought, move!"

Aaron knew enough by that point to simply run. He waved at the other drivers, who floored their vehicle and spun away from the building. Aaron dove into the driver's seat, cranked the key, and ripped away from the building. With a massive eruption, black tentacles burst out of the school wall, racing across the ground with a vengeance. They stretched outward, reaching for the van. Aaron kept his foot to the pedal, but as the tentacles began to catch up, he knew that they wouldn't be able to stay ahead for long.

"Jasper!" He called into the com as the passengers in his van screamed in fear. "Blow it! Now!"

The reply was cold and smooth. "With pleasure."

Aaron risked a glance in his rearview mirror as the school vanished in a raging inferno. The shock wave from the blast struck the van an instant later, shattering the windows and showering the refugees in glass. Aaron gripped the steering wheel tightly as the explosion continued to roar, buffering the van with wave after wave of energy.

The final blast caused the tires to skid, and nearly knocked the van off the road. Rubber screeched, and Aaron held the steering wheel tightly. Behind him, the fire was replaced by jet-black smoke, and the tentacles on the road fell dead.

For the first time that night, Aaron felt a smile creep onto his face. With a rev of the engine, they raced past the city limits and into the country. The sun was already above the horizon, shining its bright light down on the dead town. At least the light was alive.

When it came down to it, that was all he cared about.

CHAPTER 23

"Don't worry, it's okay." Inspector Birch frowned over the small clipboard. "I just want to ask some questions."

Aaron took a deep breath. "Yeah, well, it doesn't seem like it."

Birch just snorted and made a mark on the clipboard with a small pen. "Your team is the one that *enhanced* this interrogation room. You brought this on yourselves, really."

Aaron sighed and ran his hands through his hair. Upon leaving Lambspoint, before any of the vans had reached the designated drop-off point, Aaron had received a very particular call from Inspector Birch, instructing him to bring each and every survivor of the town back to Kansas City. And so, they had. And now, after close to thirty-six hours without sleep, they were all being subjected to a thorough interrogation.

Which, of course, happened to be in the same interrogation studio that Garmund and Jasper had modified to enhance terror. Lights blazed down from the ceiling, and a soft moan made the air tremble, courtesy of a series of small speakers hidden throughout the area. Fake blood and rusty tools completed the scene, no less terrifying even knowing that most of it was fake.

"Let's begin at the beginning." Birch put the clipboard down and folded his hands. "After you left, you went to a small town called Bethel, where I *believe* you blew up a warehouse and flirted with a hotel secretary. Do you care to comment?"

Aaron puffed out his cheeks. This was going to be a *long* process.

After relaying everything he could about the events, Birch sighed and finally nodded. He gestured over his shoulder, pointing to a spot in the room that Aaron couldn't see with all the lights.

"There's a chair over there." Birch chuckled darkly. "Have a seat. You can observe me, I suppose you deserve to see your team crumble."

Aaron shook his head. "You already got everything you could want from me."

"And now I need to talk to everyone else." Birch shrugged. "I *am* doing my job, a concept that you people seem completely unfamiliar with. Now, you can either take a seat while I conduct my investigation or you may wait out in the hall. Either way, things continue."

Aaron sighed and climbed to his feet. He stepped past the inspector and sat down in the secondary chair, rather amazed at how much better he could see. Birch pushed a button, and the door swung open. Jasper walked in, a smug look on his face. He glanced back and forth as he sat down, and slowly reached up to adjust his beanie.

"Jasper." Birch's voice was soft. "You were sent to this division in the first place because of suspected treason, correct?"

"I suspected someone of treason, yeah." Jasper shrugged. "Not my fault that I was suspicious of the President. Where'd Aaron go?"

"He's been disposed of." Birch growled. "Now, I have to ask you-"

"Did you drop him in the pool of acid?" Jasper crossed his arms.

Birch's eyes widened. "There's a pool of acid in this thing?"

Jasper nodded. "That little blue switch to your right. I wouldn't flip it though." He added quickly as Birch reached up to stroke the small lever. "It's rigged to have a fifty percent chance of dropping the interrogator in the acid, too."

Birch pulled his hand back like the switch was on fire. "Why would you *ever* do something like that?"

Jasper shrugged. "You know! In the movies when they have a situation where one person has to die or something or else the bad guy won't let the other person live?"

Birch just closed his eyes for a few seconds. When he spoke again, his voice was strained. "Please. Just tell me what happened last night? Were you the person who engineered those explosive drones?"

Following another significant length of time, Jasper finished his account and walked out. Garmund was next, who spent the majority of the first ten minutes expressing joy that the room was, indeed, quite terrifying. Bertha was next, who promptly spent the entire time talking about how much she had enjoyed being in the situation with Garmund, how it had brought their relationship together. Aaron was relatively certain that she was only doing so because she knew that Garmund would hack the interrogation transcripts later.

Following Bertha came Frank, who gave what was probably the most comprehensive explanation of the situation that any of them had provided. Which made sense, in a way. He *was* the security guard, after all. Aaron sat through it all, trying to keep his stomach quiet as he realized that he hadn't eaten anything in quite a good length of time. Finally, after entirely too long, Harold was called in.

Aaron leaned forward as the boy took his seat. He glanced back and forth, obviously unnerved by the room. Aaron bit his tongue trying to keep from groaning. Everyone else knew that the effects were just effects, but Harold was still in the dark about *exactly* what the Squad really was.

"Now, your name is Harold?" Birch picked up the clipboard and began making marks with his pen. Aaron frowned and leaned forward, noticing that the inspector had simply been completing a series of crossword puzzles. "You live in Lambspoint?"

"Lived." Harold glanced back and forth. "There's... There's not much left of it anymore."

"No." Birch raised his eyebrows and put the clipboard down. "I suppose not."

After a few tense seconds, Birch held up a finger. "Harold, do you know much about the people who destroyed your town?"

"They didn't destroy the town." Harold protested.

"They blew up your school." Birch shrugged. "They killed a zombie in a manner that allowed it to fall on your church, and they led the creatures on multiple destructive rampages that caused uncalculatable damage to your community. If they had never shown up, most of your people might have lived through the night, survived until morning, when the real military could have shown up."

Harold sighed. "I'm not arguing." Birch smiled softly, and Harold shrugged. "Honestly, I don't know where I stand."

"Then perhaps you could just tell me what happened." Birch folded his hands. "Explain what *actually* went down."

"I think you already have the story." Harold shook his head. "You got it from everyone else. You're just using me to try and get leverage on the squad."

Birch sighed. "Harold, let me repeat a question that I asked just above. Do you know much about the people who destroyed your town?"

Harold sighed and shook his head. "No."

"Then allow me to explain." Birch crossed his arms. "The leader, Aaron, was placed here because he failed everywhere else and happened to be the nephew of a particular general. The security guard, Frank, was placed here because he *also* failed nearly everywhere else. In fact, he was serving as a security guard for a base behind enemy lines, and fell asleep on duty. The base was stormed, and everyone died except him. The only reason he wasn't court-marshaled is due to the fact that he happens to be the *father* of a general."

Birch leaned forward. "And those are the nice ones. Jasper accused the President of treason, and tried to attack the White house using nothing but a ballpoint pen and a miniature nuclear device. He would have killed hundreds of people if he hadn't been stopped. Garmund hacked into the Pentagon and stole thousands of documents that he subsequently leaked to terrorists in exchange for money, and Bertha killed her commanding officer in cold blood after a card game went bad."

Harold closed his eyes. "Then… Why are any of them still around?"

Aaron puffed out his cheeks and tried to breathe. If he said anything, if he interrupted the interrogation, it was all over. Birch would leave with what he had, without giving Harold a chance to come around. And, at that moment, Aaron suspected that Harold was their last chance. If the boy spoke out against them, no matter how much good they had done that night, they were doomed.

"They're still around because General Herford threw his weight around." Birch snarled. "He felt bad for Aaron and Frank, and thought that the others could still be used despite the blood on their hands. They were never intended to be sent anywhere with this kind of power."

"Believe me, I can see why." Harold groaned. "They just… They portrayed themselves as our defenders!"

"And then they ruined everything." Birch egged him on.

"It doesn't matter what they did or didn't so." Harold shook his head. "They *said* that protecting the world was their job, and it wasn't."

Birch paused. "That's what you're upset about? What they *told* you?"

Harold set his jaw. "Maybe things work differently where you're from, but I come from a place where a man's word matters." He shook his head. "If you say you're going to do something, you should do it. Even Gruen *tried* to follow through with everything he said he was going to do."

"Well, farmboy, you're not in the country anymore." Birch snapped. "We care about what gets *done*, not what people say they're going to do."

Harold sighed and held up his hands. "What are you wanting from me right now?"

Birch shrugged. "I simply want the truth."

"No." Harold leaned forward, understanding dawning in his eyes. "I've heard this before. This rant, this charade."

Birch frowned down at the youth. "I'm not sure I understand."

"You're just like Gruen." Harold pressed onward. "You have all the information you need, you just need a new spin on it." He smiled slightly. "You're still not in a position of power, are you?"

Birch sputtered. "I don't know what you mean."

Harold snapped his fingers. "Yes, you do!" He grinned. "Lambspoint is a small town. Everyone knows everything that happens. The problem is when it comes to discipline. Occasionally, you have to trespass on someone's ground in order to keep the cows from getting out. Some people might get uptight about it, but the community in general will stand up for the offender.

"Now, with Gruen, it was simple." Harold stood up fully. "He was the principal, and so he should have had power. As principal, he could do almost anything he wanted. Build new rooms, move classes around, you name it. The one thing that he was almost always prevented from doing, though, was disciplining us when we did anything. Now, it's not that we *needed* it, and one time we even broke into the school late at night so we could prevent a gang from the city from wrecking everything. That said, since our parents were all on the school board, he *couldn't* do it, and that made him want to."

Harold leaned across the desk. "He would sit us down and talk to us for hours until he was able to get an angle that he could present to the board that they would accept. Right now, I think you're doing the same. You want to discipline this General Herford's unit, but you can't because you don't technically have the power. And thus, you're trying to find any sort of angle you can to take them down."

"You seem awfully confident of that." Birch blinked once. "Are you finished?"

Harold took a deep breath and nodded. "Yes."

"Good." Birch gestured at the seat. "Now please, sit down. All I want to know is whether or not the Squad destroyed your town."

Harold took a deep breath. "No."

Birch raised an eyebrow. "You're denying that the Squad took part in these activities?"

"Still trying to manipulate the situation." Harold growled. "In that case, yes. Yes, I do deny that the Squad took part in those activities. You've said it yourself, they're misfits. They stood by while *I* did all the work."

"If you're denying that the Squad did anything, then perhaps your memory should be checked." Birch smiled slightly. "We *do* have records of them doing those things." He leaned forward. "We have all the survivors of your town right here. One of them will talk. Make this easy, *boy*. Don't go to prison to protect these fools."

"I don't think I'm going to prison any more than I'm protecting those fools." Harold snorted. "I just don't like a bully. Besides, the one you *should* be going after is Incacheck. He was there, *he* was the one manipulating the zombies."

"Yes, the younger Incacheck." Birch sounded uninterested. "The others have mentioned him as well. Please forgive me if I'm less than convinced."

"You…" Harold sputtered. "You're supposed to be the government! You're supposed to be the one protecting us!"

Birch held up his hands. "I *am* protecting you."

Harold took a deep breath and climbed to his feet. "You know what?" He glared down at Birch. "Now I understand why the Squad is rogue. They *were* the ones out there protecting us, and if they weren't who they said they were, they still proved themselves. They put their lives on the line, again and again." Harold turned around. "That's more than you've done."

With that, Harold walked out of the room, banging the door behind him. Aaron groaned as Birch just chuckled and stood up.

"Well, that's one admission that you were there and participated in the destruction." Birch clapped his hands. "Why don't I bring in some food and we can continue? With luck, we'll get even better admissions of guilt from the other members of the town."

CHAPTER 24

Aaron sighed and stepped out of the interrogation room. He didn't know how long he had been in there, just that it had been a *long* time. Sleep tugged at his eyelids, trying to drag him into the darkness dancing around the edges of his vision. Outside, Garmund lay on a sleeping bag, snoring softly. The rest of the hallway was deserted, at least for that moment.

"Well, now." Birch stepped past Aaron and clapped him on the shoulder. "That was informative."

"Go to hell." Aaron muttered. It wasn't professional of him, but he didn't know what else to say. Birch had talked to each and every member of the town, and had gotten every single one of them to state that the Squad had caused damages to the town. None of the other townsfolk had even realized what they were saying, they had just gone with it.

"Now, now." Birch flashed him a small smile. "Don't be like that. Just be content with the fact that in about a month, you all will be gone, and someone competent will be working out of here."

Aaron snorted. "You're going to keep it staffed?"

"As you've been so fond of pointing out, zombies *did* just attack a small town." Birch shrugged. "We're entering a new age of warfare. Someone we can actually trust should be handed those reins."

With that, Birch sighed and stalked down the hallway. Aaron rubbed his eyes and glanced down at Garmund. He was getting ready to just walk past him when the hacker stirred and sat up.

"Oh, hey." Garmund yawned. "You're out. Frank told me to keep an eye out for you."

Aaron sighed. "Where's he at?"

"Back in the security room." Garmund climbed to his feet. "He doesn't want to leave the feed. Incacheck *did* escape, and he wants to be prepared if anything else happens."

"I suppose that's reasonable." Aaron nodded. "And everyone else?"

"In the conference room." Garmund bent down and started folding up the sleeping bag, before giving up and just leaving it lay. "They're all just waiting on you. Bertha was asleep too, last I saw. The others are trying to stay up."

Aaron sighed. "How long has it been, anyway?"

"It's currently six in the morning." Garmund shrugged and started walking down the hallway. "Almost twenty-four hours since we left Lambspoint."

"Man." Aaron rubbed his head. "I feel like I'm going to drop."

"We all do." Garmund opened the door at the end of the hallway, leading back into the office portion of the building. "Jasper cooked up something to help keep us awake. He's got a whole bunch of science mumbo-jumbo to back it up, but the point is that it works."

"That's enough for me." Aaron took the lead and walked into the conference room. Sure enough, Bertha was draped across the table, snoring loudly, while Harold and Jasper talked at the other end. In the middle of the table was a large banner that proudly read "Apocolyps Squad." Both of the awake individuals looked up as Aaron entered the room, and Jasper grabbed a nearby pitcher and started pouring a glass of a bluish liquid.

"It's a chemical sponge." Jasper started explaining, unprompted. "When you're awake, toxins build up in your body. This breaks them down just like-"

Aaron waved away the explanation. "If it works, I don't need to know how." He picked up the glass and took a deep drink. The liquid slid down his throat like snot, and he choked.

"It doesn't taste good, but it'll keep you running. At least for awhile." Jasper sighed.

"Good to know." Aaron glanced at the banner through sleep-deprived eyes. "You guys *do* know that's not how you spell 'Apocalypse,' right?"

"We were tired and thought it would be fun to make up a sign for the building." Jasper shrugged. "Harold thought it would be funny to spell it wrong, since we're sort of misfits anyway. The rest of us agreed, so there it is."

Jasper shrugged. "So, what's the news? You look like we're still being shut down."

Aaron raised his eyebrows and forced down the last of the drink. When nothing happened, he just groaned and sat down. After a few seconds, he turned to Harold.

"What are you still doing here?" He yawned, feeling a burning sensation in his lungs. "Don't you want to be with your family?"

Harold shook his head. "Birch got a hotel for all the Lambspoint people, but…" He shrugged. "I wasn't ready to go yet. I need more answers." After a moment, he snorted softly. "Besides, they were dividing rooms up via family, and Sharron probably already has Johnny Larson in there with her." At the team's blank looks, he sighed. "A guy she's had a crush on for years. I saw him in the van with her, they probably formed some sort of traumatic incident bond thing, and I don't need to be around for the kissing."

"Fair enough." Aaron certainly felt the world getting lighter, though he wasn't sure if he was *actually* getting less tired. He certainly wasn't sure what he wanted to do with Harold. Had the kid helped them in his interrogation? Or just hurt them more? It was hard to tell.

"So how bad is it?" Garmund sat down next to Aaron. "You're avoiding the question."

Aaron sighed. "It's bad." He ran his hands through his hair. "The short version of the story is that after we left, he snuck back into our headquarters and watched us via our own surveillance system. He's going to blame us for trying to fake an apocalypse, *and* for the destruction of Lambspoint. At the same time, he's going to use the evidence to get someone *better suited* to take our jobs."

Aaron shrugged. "I don't know. "We did everything we could. We saved the world, and now we're just back to where we started."

Jasper sighed and glanced down at the table. "And three of us will be executed."

Garmund took a deep breath and glanced at Bertha. "Our trials have already completed, so there won't even be any waiting." He whimpered. "I don't want to die."

Harold closed his eyes and shook his head. "But… All of you have killed before, right?"

Aaron shook his head. "Birch told you the story that Birch wanted you to hear." He groaned and ran his fingers through his hair. It was quite greasy, but it made him feel better. "Jasper uncovered evidence that the President was a Russian mole. As it turned out, he was right, but since a security guard stole his nuclear device and used it to kill several civilians, he was charged with bringing the weapon in the first place."

Garmund nodded. "I hacked the Pentagon because I was a kid in high school that didn't know any better. A kid at school challenged me to do it, so I went with it. No one *told* me that the kid was a member of a terrorist cell. Besides, I hacked the terrorist's data and erased all of it before it could be used."

Harold puffed out his cheeks. "And Bertha?"

Jasper shrugged. "No one really knows why she killed her commanding officer, but it *was* discovered later that he'd been involved in an illegal human trafficking ring for years. Bertha's actions, whether intentional or not, helped saved hundreds of people trapped in slavery overseas."

"Wow." Harold puffed out his cheeks. "That's… Why would he lie?"

"Because people are like that." Aaron sighed and frowned. HIs headache was going away, and his eyes didn't feel nearly as heavy as they once had. Interesting. "People like us. People who will do anything to get ahead in life. Even if that means ruining someone else." He sighed and turned to Harold. "And… I'm sorry."

Harold opened his mouth to reply, but Aaron cut him off. "Look, I'm not going to offer excuses. I'm not going to try and defend us, I'm not going to try and convince you that we deserve forgiveness. We were in the wrong not to tell you immediately, and for that, I apologize."

Harold let out a breath. He glanced at Jasper, who nodded. Harold folded his hands and nodded back at Aaron. "I forgive you. You *were* doing what you thought was best, and you were under a lot of pressure." He frowned after a moment, and flashed a small smile. "Now, that forgiveness comes with a catch."

Aaron caught Jasper's odd smile, and crossed his arms. "What's that catch?"

"Simple." Harold sighed. "I'm going to start my senior year here in a couple months. After that, I want to come here." He nodded at Jasper. "I've been struggling with what to do in my life after I graduate, and… Well, he's pretty dang good at chemistry. I want to move up to Kansas City and start interning with him."

Aaron raised an eyebrow. "Well, it certainly wouldn't be the most illegal thing we've ever done. Though…" He shook his head. "You do realize that we might not even be here in a year, right?"

"So we'll cross that bridge when we come to it." Harold shrugged. "Look, I saw you guys manage to kill every single zombie in an entire town just so you could escape. You just have to figure out the angle here. How do you keep your jobs? How-"

Harold was cut off by the blast of an alarm. It was the warning klaxons, the alarms that typically signaled a tight spot in a baseball game. Aaron jumped to his feet as Bertha woke up.

"Does anyone know what that alarm is?" Aaron ran out into the hallway. "Frank?"

"What's going on?" Birch walked through the doors at the end of the hallway, fire in his eyes. "I'm not gone for two seconds and you *idiots*-"

"Calling all idiots." Frank's voice blared through the speakers. "Well, idiot. And the Squad. Get into the command room, now!"

Aaron sighed and pushed past Birch, running into the monitor-filled room. As everyone else filed into the room, one by one, they began blinking to life. They all showed the same thing: The national mall, the Smithsonian, in absolute chaos. People ran back and forth, with very distinctive shambling figures wandering back and forth between the living. In the early morning light, the zombies cast long shadows across the ground, making them even more terrifying.

Aaron's jaw set. The zombies had managed to escape. They had escaped, and they have made it back to the nation's capital.

"Lark." Aaron spat. He spun to Birch and balled his fist. "Did you keep an eye on Lark?"

"Who?" Birch raised an eyebrow.

"Lark!" Aaron roared. "The Smithsonian curator that drove one of the vans back to KC!"

"Oh, yes." Birch waved his hand. "I spoke to him in the parking lot. He incriminated you quite nicely, then I allowed him to go about his business."

"You let zombies get back to the Capitol." Aaron shook his head. He didn't know *how* Lark had transmitted the creatures, but it had happened. "If you had kept him here, this would be happening where we could take care of it."

"And now the *professionals* will handle it." Birch snorted. "Once it becomes obvious that you can't be trusted with this job, your demise will come about even faster."

Aaron closed his eyes and tried to think. Maybe the Squad wasn't made of heros. Maybe they *had* lied, and maybe they had only been trying to escape Lambspoint for their own safety. That said, they were the best people to take down the zombies. And, if they wanted to keep Jasper, Garmund, and Bertha out of the electric chair, it was their only chance.

"Birch?" Aaron spun to face the increasingly steamed bureaucrat. "How did you get here?"

"Private government jet." Birch's response was quick. "Why do you-"

"We're taking it." Aaron spun to his team. "Jasper! Load the van with as much contraband weaponry as you possibly can fit. Bertha, head to the van and clean out all the fast-food wrappers. I want as much space as possible for our guns. Garmund, I want you to load up whatever portable surveillance devices you can get. Make sure Frank can tap into it from here. Oh, and get us an upgraded com system. Frank? You're staying here, keep an eye on things. Give us updates, all that kind of fun stuff. Harold?"

Harold spun towards him, an odd look on his face. "Yes?"

"Down the hall, there's a locker full of body armor."

Harold's eye lit up. "Yeah?"

"They're loaded with grenades. Strip all the grenades off them and dump the explosives into the van. Make sure you have enough for yourself."

"I'm coming too?"

"Of course." Aaron chuckled. "You wanted an internship, right? Well, we'll call Lambspoint your training, and this can be your inaugural task."

Birch sputtered. "This is most-"

"Birch?" Aaron spun towards the inspector. As the serum continued make him more and more awake, things settled into place. Things that he had forgotten about suddenly became clear. Such as the fact that he was still wearing the dueling pistols from Lambspoint. Without hesitation, he pulled one of the weapons off his chest and pointed it directly at Birch. "Your job is to shove it and stay out of the way. Tell your pilot to prep for takeoff, we need to move as soon as possible. Oh, and make sure to let the feds know that we'll be coming in hot. Actually, just let me talk to the feds."

"You think I have that kind of authority?" Birch crossed his arms. "You're digging a hole for yourself doing this!"

"The rest of my team is facing capital punishment." Aaron snarled. "If it means saving the world, I'd be happy to join them. Now, I think you have your dad's phone number." Aaron cocked the hammer of his gun. "Spit it up. Now."

"You'll regret this." Birch pulled out his phone, and Aaron shook his head. "I'll make sure you pay."

"I'll worry about that after the zombies are in the ground." Aaron snarled. "And I want the number, not the phone. You still need to call your pilot."

Birch snarled at him, but fished a business card out of his pocket and handed over the number. Aaron kept the gun pointed at Birch's chest while he pulled his cell phone out of his pocket and dialed the number. Two rings in, he heard a gruff voice on the other end of the phone.

"This is General Birch. I only give this number out to extraordinarily important people, so this had *better* be an emergency."

"It is." Aaron spoke quickly. "The zombie attack on the Smithsonian."

"We haven't confirmed that they're zombies yet." The general snapped. "I won't hear speculation until-"

"I already fought them in Kansas, so I can confirm that they're zombies." Aaron spoke quickly. "I'm calling with instructions."

"Instructions?" The general sounded almost amused. "You're going to tell me what to do? What rank are you exactly?"

Aaron tried to remember what rank exactly he had been slapped with when he was demoted. It was technically something a few ticks lower than private first class, but there was no reason to bother with such things.

"We're from a secret base in Kansas City, our clearance isn't recognized by the official system. And like I said, I've fought these things before." Aaron snapped.

"Make sure you barricade the area, prevent anything from getting out."

"Already done." General Birch's voice was getting shorter. "Unless you have something to-"

"You have to figure out where they're centered around." Aaron closed his eyes. "They'll center their activity around a specific location, probably near a large power source if there is one. If you let them get close to it, they'll evolve."

"Evolve?"

"Just trust me." Aaron shook his head. "If they hit that point, you're not keeping them inside. Trust me."

"We'll look for the patterns." The general sounded finished with the conversation. "Anything else?"

"There will be a private government jet flying over the location in about two hours." Aaron made his voice as authoritative as possible. "We're on it. Hold position until we can take care of it. Oh, and make sure we're cleared to fly through that no-fly zone over the city."

The general sounded exasperated. "Again, who are you?"

Aaron smiled as he thought about how corny the line sounded. "We're the Apocalypse Squad."

With that, he hung up, lowered the gun, and nodded at Birch, who was wringing his hands.

"You've got your jet." Birch crossed his hands behind his back. "The only reason I'm agreeing to this is because you *do* have a gun, and you seem desperate enough to use it."

"I don't rightly care what your excuse is." Aaron shrugged. "Just know that we're thankful, and the thousands of people you're saving thank you as well."

With that, he walked out the front door, where the van was nearly loaded. Jasper climbed inside the rear door, flipping the front passenger door open. Aaron jumped inside as Bertha settled in behind the wheel. He took a glance around, acknowledged that everyone was there, and nodded.

"Go. And please, make it fast."

"You boys and your speed." Bertha shook her head. "Will you ever-"

"Go!"

Bertha floored the vehicle, and they exploded out of the parking lot like a rocket. Aaron glanced in the rearview mirror to see Harold grinning like a cat. Aaron smiled back, glad the kid was enjoying himself.

They made it to the airport in record time. Aaron was quite sure that they topped one hundred thirty miles an hour on the interstate, but that was less of a concern for him. They needed to get in the air, and as quickly as was physically possible.

"So. Why are we doing this?" Harold leaned forward and yelled into Aaron's ear. "Just to get your job back? I'm fine if that's your reason, I just want to know."

Aaron bit his lip. After a moment, he sighed and nodded. "I'd be lying if I said that wasn't part of my motivation. If we don't succeed, there are good people that are going to suffer." He glanced back at Jasper, Garmund, and Bertha. After a few seconds, he sighed. "Not to mention that a lot of the logic hasn't changed since Lambspoint. If we can take them down now, it means that in six months, we can be relaxing, eating pizza instead of doing battle with an entire planet of these things."

"I suppose that's logic." Harold shrugged. "It's better than some of the logic I've heard your people spout."

"Just wait until you find out how we win Monarch games." Garmund chuckled. "Those are fun times!"

With a rush, they tore into the Kansas City airport. It took a matter of moments to flash straight past the safety barriers, ignore the tolls, and go tearing straight onto the tarmac. Aaron frowned as he glanced back and forth, trying to find Birch's plane.

"He said it would be-"

"On your right." Frank's voice echoed in their ears. "The one that looks like it has stealth technology."

"Oh, that one!" Aaron pointed towards a small jet that was covered in silver plating. "Go!"

Bertha threw the car into a gut-wrenching curve, flying towards the plane at top speed. They came screeching up to the base of the steps, the top of which held a rather concerned-looking pilot.

"We're here from Birch." Aaron yelled upwards. "You have the flight plan?"

"I have what he told me." The man yelled down. "I'm not sure this is proper, though."

Aaron turned to look at the others. "Get the van unloaded and into the plane. I'm going to let the pilot know what's happening."

There was a round of head nods, and Aaron raced up the stairs, two at a time. As he reached the top, the pilot crossed his arms. "You want to fly over the Smithsonian, which is in a strict no-fly zone."

"We're rezoning." Aaron shrugged. "The fate of the world is at hand."

"I don't care." The pilot cocked an eyebrow. "I can take you to a DC airport, but the moment we fly over the edge of the city, they'll shoot us down."

"I talked to General Birch himself." Aaron crossed his arms. "He's letting us through."

The glanced at the tarmac. "Look, I'm just a civilian that got hired because I'm better than most military pilots. I really don't feel like dying on your whim."

Aaron sighed. "What's your name?"

The man frowned. "Rodger. But-"

"Well, Rodger, there's something that you need to know." Aaron put a hand on the man's shoulder. "I've already held a gun to your boss today. You can call General Birch once we're in the air, but I *need* you in the air right now. Comprende? If our story doesn't check out, you can drop us at that point."

"Fair enough." Rodger wandered into the cockpit. "Let me know when you're ready."

Aaron ran into the plane as the rest of the team pounded up the stairs with their assorted weapons. A moment later, they were all in, and Aaron pulled the door shut tight.

"Go!" Aaron ran up to the cockpit. "Go now!"

Rodger sighed and glanced back. "If I just take off now, I might wind up breaking something critical. We could die!"

"If you don't take off now, a lot of other people will die." Aaron tapped his guns. "Now go!"

"Fine." Rodger turned stony. "Have it your way."

Aaron nodded and walked back to his seat. He had barely sat down when the plane lurched away, pressing him back into his seat. They erupted down the runway, tearing across the concrete like a rocket. He glanced out the window, wincing at the sight of several other planes flashing past a great deal closer than they probably should have been. A moment later, they were in the air.

As soon as the acceleration had worn off, Aaron walked back to the cockpit. "How long until we get there?"

"Since I'm not landing and don't have to slow down, we can be there in one hour." Rodger snapped back. "That is, of course, if your story checks out. Is that fast enough?"

"It'll have to do." Aaron nodded. "Does this plane have a stash of parachutes?"

Rodger burst out laughing. "Only two, one for me and one for Birch. You didn't bring parachutes? Boy, you guys are toast."

"We'll figure it out." Aaron turned and walked back to the squad. "Alright, what do we have?"

Jasper shrugged. "The works. Who wants what?"

Harold held up his hands. "Something less about spraying bullets and more about accuracy. Like a hunting rifle."

"I have just the thing." Jasper grabbed an oversized rifle and handed it to him. "Gas-fed plasma rifle. It takes a few seconds to recharge, but it'll melt the bone straight off any zombie we face."

"I want something that sprays a lot of bullets." Aaron held up his hand. "Most powerful machine gun you have."

Jasper grabbed a machine gun and tossed it to Aaron. "It's been modified with parts from... Well, from a lot of stuff. It has the range and power of a sniper rifle, and can crank out five rounds a second. You'll love it."

Aaron held the piece of metal, a smile growing on his face. "I think we're going to be good friends."

"Got anything with fire?" Garmund raised his hand. "I'd go for that."

"One flamethrower, coming up." Jasper chuckled and tossed him something that resembled a backpack with a fire nozzle on the end.

Bertha frowned before she chipped in. "I'd like something smaller, but with a good pop."

"I've got just the thing." Jasper pulled out a set of pistols, which he handed her. "They use gas-infused rounds, which give the bullets a little extra kick. I think you'll rather like the effects."

"And what are you saving for yourself?" Aaron raised an eyebrow. "Anything good?"

"Only the best." Jasper grinned, reached behind the seat, and pulled out a nightmareish concoction of tubes and wires. "Behold, the minimissile launcher. Complete with automatic-tracking guided missiles, a computer targeting system, and fully automatic capabilities."

Garmund practically started drooling on the plane's floor. "I want *that.*"

"You already chose fire. If you had wanted electronics, you should have asked." Jasper took a deep breath and sighed.

Aaron chuckled. "Without you, I don't know if we would have a team."

"You'd just be a bunch of losers." Jasper chuckled. "Anything we're missing?"

Aaron sighed and lowered the weapon slightly. "We're actually lacking any ability to jump out of here safely. Think you can rig up a good parachute?"

Jasper's grin split his face. "Oh, I can do one better than that."

CHAPTER 25

"What's the situation here?" General Herford leapt out of his helicopter and stalked down the street. "What resources do we have where?"

"You know, I don't think I'm obligated to tell you that." General Birch turned slowly to face Herford. "We both have three stars. You don't outrank me anymore."

"You also don't outrank me." Herford growled. "I need to know what kind of monster we're dealing with. Zombies? Vampires? Mummies? What's the deal?"

Birch groaned. "When the masses started yelling zombies, I really wasn't too concerned. The people in there, well, I've seen them. They're crazy, wild, but they're not zombies. You've got it all mixed up."

"Oh, I do?" Herford cocked an eyebrow. "Mind letting me see the action, then?"

Without waiting for an answer, Herford pushed past Birch and stalked up to the line. Army barricades had been erected on the street, locking off the road up to ten feet high. If the National Mall held what Herford feared, those walls weren't going to be nearly high enough.

A small set of temporary stairs led up the side of the wall. Herford stalked up the stairs as fast as he could, setting foot on the top with a vengeance. If Birch was going to try and keep him out, well…

What he saw took his breath away. In the exact center of the Mall was what appeared to be a mass of black tentacles. They all sprouted from a central stalk that now stretched almost fifty feet into the sky. Hundreds of tentacles stretched in all directions, forming a perimeter that stretched ever-wider as it expanded. Surrounding the tentacle monster were dozens of zombies, each standing well over thirty feet high. They were holding position, guarding the beast.

Birch joined him at the top, a frown on his face. "I assure you, we have this under control!"

"You have no idea what you're dealing with." Herford hissed. "That's a Pure Incarnation Zombie. I've only ever seen one in my entire life, and it took an army to kill it. The strike teams that you're about ready to send in are going to get slaughtered."

"How…" Birch slammed a hand down onto the top of the barrier. "Who told you my tactics?"

"No one." Herford snapped. "You're incredibly predictable. You use the same strategy on every raid you ever do, your only reason for success is that you typically have overwhelming force."

Birch shrugged. "If it isn't broken-"

"I can assure you, you won't have overwhelming force here." Herford crossed his arms. "There isn't a chance in the world of it. Have you assessed the situation at all?"

Birch raised his eyebrows. "I suppose that, given your experience with this thing, you have a weapon that can kill it?"

Herford held himself high for a moment before deflating. "I know tactics that will work better than your strike team idea, but no, I honestly don't. I have a few things I'm working on, but I wasn't expecting it so… Early."

"You were expecting this?" Birch chuckled. "You didn't bother to tell anyone that this was going to happen?"

"I rather enjoy having these stars." Herford glanced down at his shoulder. "If a soldier under your command started ranting about a zombie attack, would you have believed them?"

Birch shook his head. "No, I expect I wouldn't have." There was silence for a few moments before Birch shrugged. "If it's any consolation, we're waiting a few minutes longer. We got a call from an old military base in Kansas City. They claim to have the ability to beat this thing. We figure that if they succeed, good for them. If they don't, well, we proceed."

"Kansas City?" Herford frowned, a small seed of hope rising in his chest. "Did they say what department they were from?"

With a roar, a plane flashed over their heads, barely skimming over the level of the buildings. It banked hard as it tore over the Mall, flashing within one hundred feet of the monster. The door in the side opened, and Herford saw several figures leap out. When no parachutes deployed, a flash of fear shot through him. What were they thinking?

Flames burst from underneath all of them as some sort of propellant kicked in. The group, five in all, began to descend to the ground, riding the top of what appeared to be makeshift rockets. Herford nodded and turned to Birch.

"Apocalypse Prevention Department, isn't it?"

Recognition dawned on Birch's face, and he glowered. The face sent shivers up and down Herford's spine, a feeling of elation that he hadn't felt in a long time. Maybe things weren't as hopeless as they had seemed.

"They called themselves the Apocalypse Squad."

CHAPTER 28

Harold grinned widely as the rocket-chair he was sitting on continued to lower him to the ground. As it touched the grass, he hopped off, feeling slightly bad about how they had sliced all the seats out of Birch's private jet. Without his weight, the chair shot back up into the sky before exploding violently. Oh, well. Hopefully they would be forgiven.

"This is it." Aaron's voice echoed as the rest of the team made equally rough landings. Garmund fell on his face, while the rest of them turned to face the monster. They were there, all of them. Well, all minus Frank. "I want a count on those zombies."

"The units are still deploying." Frank's reply was instant. "Looks like about twenty, plus the giant plant thing."

"We can handle twenty." Harold grinned. "Shoot, we faced down hundreds before."

"New count." Frank's reply cut off Harold. "At least five hundred. The computer is having a hard time with the numbers."

Harold dropped the barrel of his rifle and looked up at the sky. "How do you confuse twenty with five hundred?"

"There's one huge one, twenty big ones, and a crapton of normal human ones." Frank's voice was apologetic. "Wait, now I'm reading more."

Aaron's voice growled loudly. "Where are you reading them at?"

"They're… Oh." Frank sighed. "They're in the plant. It looks like its producing them. Like a factory. They're deploying through the tentacles. First wave in twenty seconds."

"Lock and load, everyone!" Aaron planted his feet. "Get ready for the fight of your life."

Harold raised the barrel of his plasma rifle, sighting down the scope. Idly, he pointed it at the head of the nearest large zombie, which didn't seem to be in any particular hurry to attack. "Can I shoot the big one?"

Aaron chuckled. "As long as you're shooting something, I don't rightly care."

Harold shrugged and squeezed the trigger. The weapon didn't have an ounce of kick, and simply fired a blast of energy that slammed into the monster's head. It exploded quite spectacularly, and Harold smiled. "We're golden!"

Almost instantly, a new monster began to grow, expanding to half the previous size in less than ten seconds.

Harold sighed, and Aaron shook his head. "Just shoot. I think-"

With a rush, the tentacles began to disgorge zombies at a rate that Harold was certain wasn't healthy. Dozens dropped to the ground every second, turned towards the group, and tore across the ground towards them in an instant.

Aaron's gun cut loose with a vengeance, mowing down any zombie that dared cross his path. As some began to circle around the side, Garmund opened up his flamethrower, sending a purifying wash of energy that vaporized nearly all the zombies from that direction. Bertha stepped forward, pistol in each hand, firing shot after shot. Zombie head after zombie head exploded, her bullets doing a surprising amount of damage.

Jasper himself opened fire after a few moments, his rockets blowing away any and all zombies that came close. As Harold watched, several of the missiles arched over the field of battle, heading back towards the plant monster itself and detonating harmlessly against the black skin.

After a few moments of watching his new friends blast away the monsters, Harold brought the gun back up and started shooting the heads of the larger zombies. They would regrow after a few moments, but it was satisfying to see them keep dropping like that. Before long, massive bodies littered the ground, and the plant was forced to stretch its tentacles farther and farther to keep dropping new runners on solid ground.

"…shooting the big ones."

"What was that?" Harold frowned and put his finger up to his ear. It was nearly impossible to hear anything, the noise was so deafening. "Who said…"

"Keep shooting the big ones!" Frank's voice was ecstatic. "They regrow, but every time the plant has to devote energy to making a new one, it decreases runner creation by five percent!"

"That means it has a limit." Harold bit his lip. "Thanks!"

Without waiting for a reply, Harold began to squeeze the trigger faster, trying to shoot the creatures before they finished growing. He managed to fall into a rhythm that allowed him to prevent any of the creatures from reaching full size. It wasn't making any noticeable change in the number of runners coming at them, but it was something, he supposed.

After a few moments, he paused. The thing was still producing more zombies, which meant that regardless of how much power it had to spend on growing more, there was an almost unlimited energy source that it was drawing from. Somewhere, somehow...

"Frank?" Harold called out. "Can you detect any sort of power source down there?"

"Something, yeah." Frank's voice came quickly. "I can't tell you what it is, though. The kind of energy it's emitting is unlike anything I've ever seen before."

"How can I get to it?" Harold took a deep breath. "What's the fastest route?"

There was a pause. "It's at the exact center of that plant. Looks like it's being held in a giant sack just below ground level."

"How thick is the stem?"

"About thirty feet across. You would have to tunnel about ten feet horizontally and two feet down."

"I'm on it." Harold took a deep breath. "Everyone!"

"Yeah?" Aaron's voice was tight. "We're a little busy here."

"How much ammo do you have left?"

There was a pause. "Not nearly enough."

"Bertha, I need you with me. The rest of you, cover me!" Harold took a deep breath.

With a blast, he charged past Aaron, into the killing field. He could hear Aaron swearing into the com system, but he didn't care. It was him, and him alone. This would be interesting, indeed.

Ahead of him, dozens of runners began to zero in on his location. He held his rifle to his side and pulled the trigger as fast as he could, taking down or crippling a number of them. A group of them was heading in from his left when a flood of bullets cut in, rending them little more than rotting piles of flesh.

Harold grinned and pressed forward. A moment later, missiles began to arc down on his other side, keeping him clear that way. A path formed, a clear way. He simply ran, feeling an elation building in his system. With a rush, he jumped over the fallen body of one of the giants, ducked under a massive fist, and raced up to the base of the plant.

Now that he was actually at the plant, he could see that it was, like the other zombies, simply a mass of rotting flesh. Why it couldn't be a different material, he had no idea. Without a word, he dropped his plasma rifle and grabbed the grenades on his belt.

"You're awfully trusting." Bertha gasped as she ran up and started shooting backward. "If I hadn't come, you'd be dead now. They can't cover you here."

Harold shrugged and stepped out of the way so she could shoot a zombie that lurched around the base of the plant. "You're reliable. Put-"

Another zombie came around from the other direction. This one was a simple runner with a solid bone cap across its head. Bertha fired two shots that failed to breach the bone, then flipped the gun around and smashed the butt of the weapon into the creature. With a sickening crunch, the bone cap split in two, dropping the monster to the ground.

"Case in point." Harold shrugged. "Now, put five bullets into the stem, right there."

He gestured at the plant, and Bertha squeezed off five shots. The explosions blew a crack into the flesh, forming a rend almost three feet into the creature. Instantly, while Bertha went back to shooting zombies, Harold pulled the pins on three grenades and tossed them into the crack.

The rotted flesh closed over the grenades in a matter of moments. Harold smiled and counted down in his head. An instant passed, and the blast opened a massive hole in the stem. Harold glanced inside, took a deep breath, and dove inside. He heard Bertha gasp, and then he was inside the plant.

It was a gamble, he knew. If he was wrong, the flesh would close over him without a second thought, and he would be sealed inside the monster. If he was right, though, there was a chance he could land in the sack with the power source.

He landed on a surface of solid-ish flesh. His hand skidded on the slippery material, and he scrambled forward. There had to be a sack here! There just…

With a sickening schlump, the flesh under his right hand gave way, falling down into some sort of pit. Desperately, Harold grabbed at the hole, clawing it larger and pulling himself down inside. Liquid closed over his head, and he closed his eyes.

The flesh began to close behind him, and he scrambled ever faster. It began to press on his legs, preventing him from kicking. With nothing else to do, he simply pulled with his arms, dragging his head down into the sack of liquid.

The flesh pulled tightly against his torso, and he thrust forward with everything he had. Fighting every urge in his body, he opened his eyes, letting the liquid into his body.

All he could see was red. Fortunately, he could tell that it was red because of the light in front of him, shining through the liquid. He stretched his hand towards it, but found himself restrained by the flesh wall that he still hadn't quite broken through. His lungs began to burn, and he thrashed with everything he had.

Slowly, he began to pull out of the wall. His torso passed the edge... Now it was only his legs. He found himself unable to move the extensions, they were so firmly imbedded. With nothing else to do, he wrenched his torso around and began to claw at the wall. Surprisingly, he found it relatively easy to rip the flesh away from his legs, allowing him to get one leg free...

As his last leg *finally* snapped free, his lungs gave out. Instinctively, without an ounce of control on his part, he inhaled deeply. The liquid, which at that point was immediately recognizable as blood, filled his lungs. His body began to wretch, thrashing back and forth in the beast's organ.

Dimly, in the back of his mind, he recognized that he was still supposed to be doing something. Almost on their own, his hands began to open and close, grasping for… Something.

A flicker of something entered his mind as his right hand closed over something small, hard, and sharp. He didn't have time to register what it was before a sense of falling rushed through his system. Light flooded his eyes, and he felt himself carried away.

CHAPTER 27

"Whatever that kid is doing, I sure hope he does it quickly!" Garmund called out as he kept pouring flame into the hoard of zombies. "I'm about out!"

"I just hope he's okay." Jasper muttered. "If something happens to him-"

Aaron nodded. "Just keep shooting. We count our losses after the fact."

With a massive whoosh, the plant froze, twisted, and collapsed on itself. The tentacles turned to dust as they collapsed downward, filling the area with a massive cloud. The attacking zombies simply dropped, transforming into what they were: corpses. The monstrous creatures landed simultaneously, shaking the Mall with their massive thuds.

Aaron took his fingers off the trigger of his gun, feeling a moment of shock. It only lasted a moment, though, as Jasper tore past him and flew across the grass, running towards the location where the plant had once stood.

Aaron followed closely, running as fast as he could, though that wasn't saying much. To say that the Mall was a disaster was an understatement. Bodies were strewn so thickly across the ground that it was nearly impossible to run. Aaron found himself having to almost hop across the expanse, trying to avoid stepping on anything dead. Pools of blood and rotting bodily fluids filled the gaps between the bodies, creating a disgusting slick of gunk that nearly caused him to slip and fall more than once. Jasper ran far faster than Aaron did, seemingly content with stepping on the corpses. He *did* actually fall, though he jumped immediately back to his feet.

Finally, after far too long, they drew up to the base of a massive hole in the ground. It was close to one hundred feet across, and seemingly as deep. Bertha was already inside, sliding down the quite steep wall. Jasper dropped to the ground and jumped into the pit, sliding straight past Bertha. Aaron held his breath and simply watched as both of them made their way to the bottom, where a very limp Harold lay sprawled on the exposed dirt.

Jasper reached him an instant before Bertha, knelt down next to him, and grabbed his wrist. A moment passed, and Jasper stood back up. His head was drooped, and Aaron felt like someone had just hit him in the gut. He took a deep breath and sat down at the edge of the crater. Bertha knelt down next to Harold as well, placing her fingers on his throat. Her slumped posture as she stood back up was all that Aaron needed to know.

The smalltown farmboy had been the one to save them all. Imagine that.

Aaron swore as he turned away. Harold had been the soul of the team, for the short time he had been there. Aaron had drug him along on a mission to Washington DC to take on a bunch of zombies. Who *did* that? And better yet, who *agreed* to do something like that? Harold had been a unique individual, worthy of songs and poems in his memory.

"Hey!" Jasper's surprised yell cut through the silence. Aaron ran back to the edge to see Harold on his feet, looking more than slightly embarrassed to be hugged by Jasper in public. After a moment, he hugged him back, and Jasper started helping him back to the edge of the crater.

It took almost five minutes to get Harold out of the crater. Both Jasper and Bertha working together could barely get him up, Harold simply didn't have any energy by himself. When he finally got to the top, Aaron grinned helped pull him over the edge and patted him on the back.

"I don't know what you did, but you did it good."

"Thanks." Harold chuckled, turned, and helped pull Jasper up out of the pit. "I'm not sure quite what I did, either. Hey, it worked!"

"That's true." Aaron chuckled as Bertha climbed out as well. "Just... Thanks."

"No problem." Harold crossed his arms and grinned at Jasper "I had to make sure I would be initiated for good. Self-sacrifice is the best way to do that, isn't it?"

"Typically." Aaron laughed. "Ahh, you're good, you know that?"

"I get the feeling that *he* isn't going to feel that way." Harold pointed across the grass. Aaron turned to see a general and a contingent of troops making their way across the area.

As the general drew close, Aaron braced himself. The facial features were fantastically similar to their pesky inspector. This was very obviously General Birch, and he didn't look happy in the slightest.

"Apocalypse Squad, huh?" General Birch crossed his arms as he showed up. "You know good and well that that isn't an official military name. I also have it on good authority that this boy here isn't military and has no business operating in military business."

Aaron held up his hand. "I feel the important part is that we killed the big monster that was about ready to kill the capitol. Anyone disagree?"

"You commandeered a military jet, flew into a no-fly zone, threatened military officers, held a gun to *my son,* and I'd be willing to bet that these weapons aren't legal." Birch crossed his arms. "Am I wrong?"

Aaron sighed. They were already toast. If he was going to go out, he was going to do it with as many insults as possible. "Look, let's be real. You're sore that we got the trophy and you didn't."

"I-"

"The guy's got you there." General Herford, Uncle Bruce, materialized behind Birch and clapped him on the shoulder. "Be realistic. They did what you and I failed to do, and they did it without any major resources. You can't say a word, and you know it."

Birch opened his mouth, and Bruce Herford held up his hand. "Aaron Herford, I hereby promote you to the rank of colonel, effective immediately. Your troops will also be given field promotions. The new boy is hereby conscripted into the military and given the same rank. Additionally, your pay will be raised and your facilities upgraded accordingly."

"You can't do that!" Birch fumed.

"Actually, I can." Herford chuckled. "Oh, and I feel I should point something out. Since I spoke first, and we're the same rank, you can't countermand my orders."

Birch fumed. "I'll talk faster next time."

"You do that." Herford patted Birch on the shoulder as the man stalked away. Aaron spread his arms, but his uncle held up a finger. "I'm terribly sorry. I know you must have questions, and I want to answer them. Believe me, I'll get around to it as quickly as I can. Right now, all you can do is go back to your facility and get ready."

Aaron frowned. "Ready for what?"

His uncle smiled, a gleam in his eye. "Whatever comes next."

As his uncle swept away, Aaron took a deep breath. There was a sense of finality that came with this monster's defeat. Whatever Harold had done, Aaron was quite certain that the threat was passed. They were free, well and truly.

They were the Apocolyps Squad.

CHAPTER 28

Herford walked into his office, a grin on his face. Birch had been put in his place, perhaps for good. Herford's team, so long in the making, was functioning fantastically. It was time for a celebration. He had a two-hundred-year-old bottle of scotch in his safe, saved for such an occasion. Or, at the least, saved for the end of the world.

The moment the door was shut, a shadow materialized from behind his desk. Herford crossed his arms and cocked an eyebrow.

"What would you have done if it wasn't me?"

"Killed you." Donald Incacheck placed a small pistol on his desk and sat down in the general's chair. "I figured that a meeting would be in place about now."

"I thought the same thing." Herford sighed. "First, out of my chair."

"No!" Incacheck crossed his arms and stuck out his bottom lip. Herford just crossed his arms and stared at the insane scientist until Incacheck finally sighed and climbed to his feet. Herford slid around to the backside of the desk and sat down, while Incacheck stomped around the desk like an angry toddler and dropped into a guest chair. For a few moments, they just stared at each other.

"I wasn't expecting it to begin so soon." Herford finally broke the silence.

"Neither was I!" Dr. Incacheck leaned forward and pointed a finger at Herford. "When my sensors registered the effects of the stone beginning, I made my way to the town. Your little team almost screwed it up for all of us."

"Really?" Herford raised his eyebrows. "I was under the impression they did quite a fantastic job."

"They did a fantastic job of mucking *everything* up." Incacheck threw up his hands. "I was set up in the church of the town, working on an inoculant for the disease. Not just an inoculant for *that* disease, but a preventative measure for all future encounters with these powers! They destroyed all my work and let all my test subjects loose."

"Yes." Herford sighed and leaned back in his chair. "I was hoping to ask you about that. My nephew tells me that you told them that you were working on an evolutionary virus that would affect all of humanity? That you bragged about causing the zombie outbreak in the first place?"

"If someone thinks that I'm capable of such a thing, I have to foster those rumors!" Incacheck nearly jumped out of the chair. His hands spun like pinwheels, and he leaned forward. "Everyone thinks I'm a joke! I had a chance to do some true evil!" After a few more second of silence, he closed his eyes and shrugged. "Besides, if I had told them I was working on a cure, they wouldn't have believed it. They might have even just shot me for impudence. And believe me, I would *not* look good in a casket."

Herford raised an eyebrow. "And did the people you tested the cure on manage to survive?"

Incacheck shook his head wildly, sending his hair flapping in the wind. "By the time I finished, the zombies had evolved far enough that it would have taken a suit of armor to survive those bites, virus or no virus. The worst part of the whole ordeal was that your team managed to take down my force field. If they hadn't managed to kill all the zombies, the creatures might have escaped!"

"The zombies *did* escape, and my team handled it just fine." Herford sighed and closed his eyes. He was beginning to remember why he had hidden the bottle of scotch in the room to begin with. Because he had known that dealing with Incacheck on a more regular basis was going to be *insufferable*. "Their methods are a bit abnormal, I'll admit. However, I'll also say that they haven't actually been told what's happening yet. They went to the town because they were tracking you."

"Believe me, I won't be so obvious next time." Incacheck growled. "If they would have just bowed to my will, we could have ended the threat in a matter of hours. Instead, we worked against each other and destroyed the entire city."

"You also didn't really give them a chance to help you. In any event, it worked out alright in the end." Herford shrugged. "It gave them the confidence and manpower to take the beast down when the shard was accidentally taken back to the capitol."

"Yes. I saw that. Miserable incompetents." Incacheck balled his fists. "Well, now that we're done recapping the past, are you ready to face the future?"

"Not just yet." Herford held up his hands. "Jim Paulo dealt with this thing the last time it reared its head. He never mentioned the zombies growing, evolving. What happened there?"

"That much, I actually can tell you!" Incacheck laughed. "Another shining example of how your team nearly got us all killed! How can I explain it in terms simple enough for your pathetic mind?" Incacheck scratched his head in thought. "The shard can emit a certain amount of energy. That energy can manifest itself in all dead bodies within a certain radius."

"Following so far." Herford nodded. "Continue."

"Alright." Incacheck frowned. "Let's use a metaphor. We'll represent the shard's energy as pennies." Incheck pulled several pennies out of his pocket and dropped them onto the desk. "You start out with ten zombies and ten pennies. The shard is powering all the zombies normally. Well, then one zombie gets shot." Incacheck picked up a penny and dropped it on top of another nearby coin. "You now have nine zombies, but you still have ten pennies. So, one zombie now has two pennies, giving it the ability to run and sprint. You kill *that* one, and now another zombie has three pennies."

He shook his head as Herford began to frown. "The point is that, as you kill more and more zombies, the energy gets more and more concentrated. If the dead had risen, and no one in town had fired a single shot, never killed a single zombie, the undead would have been so weak they couldn't have broken through plastic wrap. Everyone would have survived, and I could have finished my research."

"Makes sense." Herford knit his brow as he tried to follow the logic. "What happened in DC, then? The city's filled with cemeteries it could have raised, why create just one monster?"

"It learned." Incacheck chuckled softly. "It learned even faster than your *stupid* team did! The shard has a brain!" He cackled for a few seconds before sighing. "Speaking of the shard, I assume that it's in a safe place?"

Herford bit his lips. He knew that the squad had taken it, but he didn't know if they had put it in a safe or thrown it in the trash. "Yep, it's safe."

"Good." Incacheck nodded and stood up. "I suggest you get it to me as soon as possible so I can start working on a way to destroy it."

"I'll get it to you as soon as I can." Herford shrugged. "So. The future."

"Yes!" Incacheck tilted his head back and laughed for several long seconds. Herford had no idea *what* he was laughing at, which made it even more eerie. "I have my network of sensors nearly operational. If I push hard, another few months of travel should allow me to pinpoint any and all shards throughout the world the moment that they activate."

"And once you have it up and running?"

"Your squad was to be a booster to my efforts. They were meant to compliment me!" Incacheck stood up grandly and walked towards the door. "I need assurance that your team isn't going to run all over me again. I need their full compliance! I need their loyalty! Explain it to them however you want, just make sure that they know that the younger Incacheck is a good guy." He paused for a moment, then chuckled. "At least, let them know I'm not trying to kill them."

"I can't promise how they'll take it." Herford shrugged. "But yes, I'll pass it along."

"Good." Incacheck held up a finger. "Also, start working on a way to deploy them faster. We need to be at any location in the world within a matter of three hours."

Herford held up his hand. "I'll work on it."

"Good." Incacheck took a deep breath, once again suddenly gaining a veneer of sanity. "Last thing. You think you can send a few nukes towards South America?"

"Not a chance." Herford shook his head. "We can't make any more moves against the your father until we know for sure where he's weak. If we send them down, and he just sends them back, we'll be in even more trouble than we are now. We need a good reason to move against him."

"He's murdered millions of people." Incacheck held up his hands. "That's reason enough!"

"You don't exactly have the cleanest hands in that respect." Herford leveled his gaze at the scientist.

Incacheck chuckled softly. "I suppose you're right. Well, I'll be seeing you then. Just promise me something. If you see my father face to face, put a bullet through his head before he returns the favor."

Herford chuckled. "Without hesitating."

"Good." Incacheck nodded. "Our business is concluded. I'll see you again once my network is in place."

The scientist vanished, and Herford chuckled for a moment at just how ironic his life truly was. He was working with a wanted murderer to take down… Shards. Evil shards, but that's really all they were when it came down to it.

Slowly, he forced himself to his feet and walked towards his safe. He hesitated at the keypad, his fingers just brushing against the keys. The world was ending, the dead were rising. Who knew what monsters lay around the corner? If ever there was a time for a drink, it was at that moment.

With a sigh, Herford lowered his hand, turned, and stalked over to his personnel files. If his squad was going to succeed, they needed someone who knew airplanes and experimental technology. If he wasn't mistaken, he knew just the person. All it would take was a phone call.

CHAPTER 29

"Can I come in?" Harold knocked on Jasper's door. "It's Harold."

"Of course!" The door swung wide open as Jasper pulled it back with a flourish. "Come on in! What's on your mind?"

Harold took a deep breath as he stepped inside Jasper's workroom. Benches ran around the edge of the entire wall, all of which were covered in dismantled weaponry. A chemistry table filled the far wall, and boxes of components sat on shelves that surrounded the area.

Jasper shut the door behind him and walked around to his chemistry set. "You want to see what I'm working on? I'd love to get your opinion!"

"Jasper?" Harold bit his lip. "I know how you do it."

"Do what?" Jasper chuckled. "I don't know what you're talking about."

Harold pulled a small shard out of his pocket. It was the exact same as when he had seen it in the Smithsonian exhibit. Engraved with that single symbol, a drawn bow.

"I got to thinking about it after my conversation with Lark. You always know how to make weapons from nothing. Everyone else is amazed at your talent, but I've seen what you do. I've seen how *I've* created acid from nothing but floor dust and metal shavings. That's no ordinary chemistry." Harold tapped the shard against his palm. "This shard is part of the Philosopher's Stone. Lark mentioned believing that it might actually be real. *That's* how you work your magic."

Jasper shrugged. "You've got me."

Harold frowned. "You're not going to argue?"

"Honestly, it's kind of fun to tell someone." Jasper chuckled. "The philosophers of old used to dream about changing lead into gold. The stone could be a source of unlimited wealth. I find it much easier and useful to use it for a source of unlimited PETN. You know how to work the techniques correctly, you can turn anything into pretty much anything. Pretty nice, huh?"

"Yeah, I suppose so." Harold frowned. "I just… I have a few questions."

"Fire away!" Jasper adjusted his beanie and leaned against the wall.

"You don't actually *have* a shard." Harold held up the small piece of stone. "And yet, you can use alchemical techniques. How?"

"That much is actually pretty simple." Jasper grinned and held out his hand. "May I?" Harold dropped the shard into Jasper's palm, and the weapons expert grinned. "There have been stories passed through my family for generations. There was supposedly a tablet, a rock composed of glyphs that could move, that could show you exactly how to create anything you want. The tablet was destroyed by those who feared the power of alchemy, but enough techniques had been written down that we've been able to continue the craft through the years." Jasper's eyes went wide. "You said you think this thing was a piece of that actual tablet?"

"That's my best bet." Harold shrugged. "Lark mentioned it being found by the body of a Spanish missionary. Jim Paulo? The zombie guy? Any coincidence that I happened to find this shard inside the giant tentacle monster?"

Jasper bit his lip. "So that's how you managed to kill it. It was using that shard as a power source."

Harold nodded and took the shard back from Jasper. "Yep. Again, that's my best bet. When I grabbed it, the whole thing turned to dust."

"Did it show you anything?" Jasper narrowed his eyes. "Any images, techniques, guides?" He shrugged. "You just sound like you know more than you're letting on."

Harold sighed and nodded. "In the few seconds after I grabbed it, I got a slideshow of images. People reading the tablet, using techniques, all the way back to the guys that carved it. I even saw you in that chemistry lab. The shard must be proud of you."

Jasper's eyes fill with water. "I think that's the nicest thing anyone's ever said to me." He took a deep breath. "Wow. I bet that sucked the air out of your lungs."

"Funny thing." Harold chuckled. "It actually did. See, I've been having a hard time breathing ever since that event."

Jasper's eyes narrowed, and he took a step closer. "What do you mean?"

"I've also been having a rather difficult time bleeding." Harold picked up a knife off a nearby table and drove it through his arm. It felt… Well, it rather tickled, but there wasn't a bit of pain. Harold pulled it out, watching in fascination as the flesh simply healed.

"WHAT?!" Jasper jumped back, eyes wide. "You're a zombie!"

"Could you keep it down?" Harold hissed. "You'll let everyone else on the base know about it!"

"Everyone else in the base is watching that new superhero movie in the command room." Jasper didn't take his eyes off Harold's arm. "Why aren't you trying to eat me?"

"I don't know."

"Why can you talk?"

"I don't know."

"Why aren't you rotting?"

"I don't know!" Harold laughed and shook his head. "You're taking this harder than I am. Do you have *any* idea how hard it was to get up out of that crater with you and Bertha all over me? I thought for sure one of you was going to take my pulse."

"I was too busy being glad you were alive!" Jasper was still wide-eyed. "Except that now you're not. Except you are. This is weird. You're a *zombie!*"

"I get the feeling that we're going to be having a lot of weird things happening." Harold shrugged. "One of the things I saw was the tablet being shattered. Jim Paulo may have carried this shard with him over from England, but it's far from the only piece of the philosopher's stone left on the planet."

Jasper's eyes flashed. "You think you can pinpoint a few of the shards?"

"In topographical detail." Harold nodded. "Here's the kicker. These things, all the shards, possess an enormous amount of energy. And they're all about ready to pop. One right after another."

Jasper frowned. "What are we going to do? Should we tell the others?"

Harold bit his lip. After all his tirades about being a man of his word, after all his rants about how the Squad should have told him what they truly were… In that moment, he understood it perfectly. "Not if I have anything to say about it." Harold waved his hand. "What am I going to tell them? I'm a zombie and Jasper builds his weapons using the thing that transformed me into a zombie? Oh, and all that energy is about to destroy the world again?"

"I get the picture." Jasper held up his hand. "What do you think we should do, then?"

Harold grinned. Finally, the point of the conversation was here. "I want you teach me. I want to know how to use the stone."

Jasper grinned brightly. "We'll begin immediately."

Coming soon:

Apocolyps Squad II

Fall 2019

For more great content, check out
www.leadpyramidpublishing.com

The Eternal Quest

An orc, a dwarf, and an elf walk into a bar.
What happens next?

Volume 1: Shadows of the Wondrisil
*Three adventurers find themselves meeting in a small, unassuming
coastal town in Donisil. After finding a magical book, they are
thrown into a mad hunt for a mysterious race of beings…*

Appendix A: Blood and Water
*Ready to be done with Donisil, Talfin returns to his home country of
Tifingor. However, things aren't quite as he left them…*

Volume 2: Beings of Light
*The new team heads north, looking for answers. While none present
themselves, they begin to realize that their actions were a bit more far-
reaching than they had anticipated…*

New chapters release every single week! Only available
through www.leadpyramidpublishing.com

www.ingramcontent.com/pod-product-compliance
Lightning Source LLC
Chambersburg PA
CBHW020321200626
46814CB00006BB/2356